GO THERE.

OTHER TITLES AVAILABLE FROM **PUSH**

W9-ASK-647

DIRTY LIAR

BRIAN JAMES

SCHOLASTIC INC.

NEW YORK   TORONTO   LONDON   AUCKLAND   SYDNEY

MEXICO CITY   NEW DELHI   HONG KONG   BUENOS AIRES

ISBN 0-439-79623-7

All rights reserved. Published by PUSH, an imprint of Scholastic Inc., 557 Broadway, New York, NY 10012.

SCHOLASTIC and associated logos are trademarks and/or registered trademarks of Scholastic Inc.

Library of Congress Cataloging-in-Publication Data

James, Brian, 1976–
Dirty liar / Brian James.
p. cm.
Summary: No longer able to tolerate living with his alcoholic mother and her abusive boyfriend, high schooler Benji, nicknamed Dogboy, has moved in with his emotionally distant father, stepmother, and stepsister, and strives to be invisible at home and at school until a series of events forces him to express himself.
ISBN 0-439-79623-7 (hardcover)
[1. Emotional problems—Fiction. 2. Self-esteem—Fiction. 3. Family problems—Fiction. 4. Interpersonal relations—Fiction. 5. High schools—Fiction. 6. Schools—Fiction.] I. Title.
PZ7.J153585Dir 2006
[Fic]—dc22   2005008727

12 11 10 9 8 7 6 5 4 3 2 1   6 7 8 9 10 11/0

Printed in the U.S.A.   40
First printing, February 2006

For Everyone Else Who Shares This Story

ACKNOWLEDGMENTS

Chris P.—for being my friend when I didn't have any.

John Frusciante—whose music inspires me to be a better person.

Oana Ban—for my interest in gymnastics.

Richey Manic—whose words and disappearance haunt me.

Doggie—forever my faithful cat.

David—for being the only one I'd trust with this story.

My Family—for always being there to support me.

My wife, Sarah—who will always be my angel.

DIRTY
LIAR

I've been taught to kill and fight this,
to bury it deeper where nobody could find it,
because nobody wanted to know.
–W. Axl Rose

Deep Inside We're All Somebody

I am nothing to them.

I'm only a list of differences . . a list of adjectives to describe what they see when they look at me . . a collection of words to define themselves as whatever I am not.

Strange . . because they say so.

Weird . . because they say so.

Troubled.

Broken.

The world is happier if I never get fixed because trash is better left out by the side of the road. No one minds the smell or the maggots as long it stays out of sight and far away.

I try to stay as far from everyone as possible. I walk near the edges of the hallways. I sit in the back row of every class. I keep hidden behind my hair which I've let grow long so that it covers my face. I figure if they don't want me then I don't want them.

They say they are *concerned* about me. Everyone has been *concerned* about me my whole life. My teachers . . my guidance counselors . . my father and stepmom . . concerned that I don't fit in . . concerned that I don't reach out and embrace being popular or having lots of friends . . concerned that I don't want any of the things they want for me to want. That is what makes me strange and dangerous to them.

They are concerned about my silence.

They want me to talk about what's inside of me.

–I don't understand you– my dad says whenever I sit there facing the wall . . the color of my eyes like worn-out blue jeans behind the bleached strands of hair . . a tiger behind the cover of trees . . fierce and protected. *–I don't know why you have to be so goddamned difficult all the time.*

I want to tell him there is nothing difficult about silence.

Staying silent is better than conversation.

Staying silent is better than telling the truth.

Besides . . they don't really want to know what I feel. They don't want to hear the truth because it upsets them. They don't want to hear about how my mother says I ruined her life . . that I cause her to drink. They don't want to hear about that asshole boyfriend of hers. Roy. They don't really want me to tell them about how he thought I

4

was *pretty for a boy* . . or how his hand felt like burning liquid as it moved down my spine . . how his fist felt like metal when I tried to pull away from him.

That would make them uncomfortable.

That would damage their view of the world.

They only want to know what happens if it happens according to their rules for how things are supposed to be. Anything that creeps in to ruin the illusion of nice homes and big cars and shopping malls needs to be kept inside . . buried away . . lost and better forgotten. But all I see when I look around are the bad things that have crept in . . the demons that live near the shadows where I stay. I can't see the things they do . . so I stay silent as much as possible.

I've learned to lie.

I've learned to say *–fine–* to any question about how I feel.

Because nobody cares if I'm well only if I behave well . . only if I'm normal. And that is why they are concerned. Because I'm not normal. I don't dress normal. I don't wear my hair normal. I don't say normal things like the other kids in the hallways do. And I wish they'd see that. I wish they'd stop being so fucking concerned and leave me alone.

–You just do it for attention.– I've heard them say that . . the girls with their matching clothes and matching haircuts and matching faces. *–You just want to be different*

5

that's all.– They think they're so fucking clever and smart . . that they've figured out some gimmick I've come up with to make people notice me.

–That's it all right you caught me– I usually snicker back at them and give them a big FUCK YOU smile to see them on their way.

My stepmom would ask why I have to be so angry . . why can't I be more polite and try to make them understand me. But how do I make them understand that nothing I do is to get attention . . that everything I do is the opposite? How do I explain to them that I learned when I was young not to seek attention . . that whenever I did something like that my mom would hate me . . *–Think you're so fucking cute–* she would say . . wiping the smile from my face with the long fingernails she would spend every Saturday night painting and filing in front of the television before her dates arrived.

I don't want their attention.

I want only to disappear . . to blend in with the demons so that they won't see me and won't come inside anymore to hurt me.

It seems to be working. I've only been at this school for two months and already the majority of kids seem uninterested in me . . content to label me one of the freaks . . to ignore me as long as I stay out of sight.

We stick together. The freaks. We understand each

6

other enough to know that we are all misunderstood. We find each other easily . . we share the same spaces on the outer edges of high school society. We meet in the shadows. We watch each other's backs. We stay united in our hatred of everything and take comfort in a shared sadness because at least that is ours . . at least no one else can take part in that.

We are nothing to them and no one else is anything to us.

–Working on your fucking masterpiece?– Sean says to me . . leaning in close to me so that his words are like a winter storm that blows in late in the season . . something that I can feel in the center of my bones more clearly than I can hear.

–Just making some notes– I say and quickly close the notebook where I write everything . . pages and pages of scribbled thoughts that read like pieces of a shattered window. I hope that one day I will read them and that I will be able to put them together so that they make sense to me.

–Whatever– Sean says and sits in the chair next to me. He stands out among all the bright nauseating colors of the cafeteria. His black t-shirt and black jeans . . hair black like the color of a black magic marker and skin like the color of ghosts. He is like a sickness in the room . . the orange chairs and green tables join forces with the yellow walls and red

8

floors trying to reject him the way blood cells reject para-sites in the body.

Sean doesn't say anything else.

He stares far away at nothing.

I don't know if he is waiting for me to say something or if he is content in stillness. I haven't known him long enough to be able to pick up on what he's thinking. His expression hardly changes so it's not easy to read. Like the eyes of rabbits and birds his eyes never show anything going on inside. The perfect demon disguise . . the perfect way to go unnoticed by them.

There is something completely insane about him. He can sit there and be almost perfectly still and then suddenly twitch to life like the wiring in his brain is all short-circuited. That's when there are sparks in his eyes like the reflection of sunlight. He becomes animated . . uncontrolled . . alive.

It's what makes him an outcast like me.

It's what makes the other kids frightened of him.

And it's what makes us friends because we can under-stand each other because we are both damaged according to everyone else. We are fine with each of us being the way we are . . we are not concerned about it . . we are not trying to fix anything.

–*You still coming after school today Dogboy?*– he says . . speaking to the wall . . expression never changing. It is one of his low-voltage sparks . . where his mouth moves and the words come out but it looks like he never moved. I wouldn't have known he was talking to me if he'd hadn't said my name.

Dogboy.

A nickname that I've had since I was young. I used to hate it. I used to cry on the playground when they'd chant *Dog-Boy Dog-Boy* and get sand in my mouth and in my eyes where the tears were.

I don't hate it so much anymore. It fits me. It's the name I use. It's the name I've adopted because I am like a mutt that doesn't have a home . . that wanders around for scraps of affection. Dirty and scrawny. But dangerous too. A low warning growl always deep in my throat and unpredictable when I might bite.

I am Dogboy more than I am Benji.

Nobody calls me Benji except my family and my girl-friend Lacie. But she's far away now . . and I don't speak much to my family . . so really I'm not sure how long before Benji disappears. I don't know that I don't want him to disappear . . to die . . to become so small inside me that I can't find him anymore even when I search for him.

–I guess so– I say.

Sean nods. Slowly. Biting his lower lip and nodding . . transforming my answer into a yes by contemplating it over and over again. *–We'll meet in front of the North Gym. Keith'll be there too.–*

–All right . . that's cool– I say.

Outside the clouds are getting heavier. The sunlight is erased from the wall by a shadow that moves fast and deliberate. The rain will start to fall soon. The ground will be wet in the woods after school when we leave. The new grass will be soft under our shoes . . they'll make no sound as we move between the trees like moving through dreams. The rain will hide our tracks.

The fluorescent light seems brighter without the sunlight . . burning off the color in the room like fog burning off on a hot morning. It makes the outline of everything seem stronger. Sean seems to fade into the whiteness . . the electricity erases the paleness of his skin the way the shadows erase the sun. When I look at him I only see the outlines . . the strands of his hair like black flames that sit over the clean-shaven parts of his now invisible head.

–I'll see you then man. I gotta run– he says . . springing to his feet in one of his spasms of motion. I nod to him and watch his clothes walk away . . squinting my eyes to see if I can make him completely disappear.

Then I return to my notebook. I begin writing down the pieces of conversations that are happening around me. A phrase from this one . . a word from another . . recording what I hear and collecting more fragments that someday I will put together in order to see my reflection.

Tuesday 2:15 pm

There's something about Rianna Moore that reminds me of Lacie.

It has nothing to do with the way she stands or the way she talks. They look nothing alike. Her hair is more the color of dirty sunshine than the color of midnight. Not as curly either. Not as clean. And there is nothing shy about her the way there is about Lacie.

But their eyes are the same.

Both of them hide secrets behind their eyes.

She smiles a lot. She smiles at nothing at all . . smiling when she thinks no one is looking at her. There is nothing friendly in her smile. Her smile is the way she hides from the demons.

I watch her every day in class. I listen as she talks to her friends . . the way she says things that make them laugh but they don't seem to notice that she never laughs along. They don't seem to notice that she wears the same four shirts every week and that she chooses a different one to wear twice . . or that her sneakers are the cheaper version of their own . . or that she carries her books in her arms and not in a backpack.

I notice.

I see that she doesn't really fit in with them . . with the kids who buy the newest of everything . . who drive cars that are better than any car my mom's ever driven . . that they get whatever they want simply by frowning . . that they don't have to ask and that they certainly don't have to say thank you.

They will notice it too.

Soon.

Because those things seem to matter more each year of high school that goes by. Those things that didn't mean shit when we were little slowly become the things that define us . . that decide who we can and who we cannot be friends with . . that determine which fake label gets stuck to us like price tags on items in a store.

I know because my mom and I didn't live in a house.

I know because we lived in a trailer park on the far end of town.

I had friends who wouldn't come to see me because they didn't want to be seen there . . in *Tricia Meadows . . Tricia Ghettos.* My friend Avery would drive me home sometimes but would drop me off on the road because he wouldn't want to come in. I guess he thought being poor was contagious . . before you know it you are the one wearing last year's fashions and skipping lunch because you don't want to be seen eating something you found in the back of the refrigerator.

Rianna is more like me than she knows. Her friends just haven't noticed it yet. Or maybe they have and are only letting her hang on . . maybe they have only noticed behind her back for now. But when they do decide they don't want her around they will push her to the side because she is trash like me only she is trash wrapped like a Christmas present. When they see what's inside they will throw the present out with the wrapping paper.

I've tried to find out about her.

I asked Sean about her but he didn't say much. *–I don't know . . I had like second grade with her. She's a little too popular for my taste.–* And I said *–oh–* and *–yeah–* and other things that made it sound like I wasn't interested.

I have my last class with her at the end of every day. I've tried following her after . . staying a little way behind her in the hallway so I could see which bus she took home because I thought if maybe I could see the house where she lives that somehow it would give us something in common . . but she stayed after school for something and I had to catch my bus.

I try to plan where I sit . . getting to class early so that I can guess where I think she will sit. Somewhere by the windows. She always sits by the windows so she has something to entertain her when class begins.

I usually try to sit in the back row . . two rows over from the window. I usually keep my fingers crossed that she will sit three seats away from me diagonally.

Today I move closer.

I am late and she is early and the only seat left is right next to her but behind one person.

I try not to look at her as much. It feels dangerous to stare being this close. But there's something about the way she moves that demands to be looked at. The way her hand comes up to tuck her hair behind her ears . . the bend of her arm . . the angle of her elbow to her wrist and the easy way in which she brings it down again like a ballerina in a heavy gray sweatshirt that fits her too big.

It's not Rianna who catches me. It's her friend.

That's the problem with being so close . . it becomes obvious to other people who you are staring at. And when her friend leans forward and taps Rianna on the shoulder I know I've been caught and quickly turn away.

My hair hanging in front of my face isn't enough to hide behind and I can feel my face turning pink with a heat that is like standing in front of an open oven.

Her friend whispers.

Points.

Laughs and sits back down and I can feel Rianna's eyes studying me . . eyes that are like stars submerged in tropical green water.

Her hand reaches up to tuck her hair behind her ear again . . and she pauses. I look over quickly and she half smiles so that the freckles disappear on the left side of her face before we both turn away and pretend to watch the blackboard.

When class ends I don't wait for her to leave like I usually do. I want to get out of there before her. I want to be halfway home before she and her friend have time to close their books.

I push past the stupid girl in front of me who refuses to hurry. –*Watch it creep*– she says. I wink and give her a quick hand gesture that I doubt she could interpret as a wave.

Probably shouldn't have . . because her asshole jock friends see it. They stand in front of the door to block me . . arms folded in front them . . planted as firm as two thick trees only without the brains that trees have.

–*Gotta get somewhere?*– one says . . and I toss my head back so that I can see them more clearly. I know that Rianna is watching me from over by the windows and I wish these guys would just fucking move. I mean what do they have to prove? That they can beat the shit out me?

17

Well no shit they can!

I know I'm not strong. I know they're bigger and tougher than me. Everyone fucking does! So they need to prove it to who?

–Come on . . move– I say . . trying hard to sound apologetic and serious . . trying not to sound nervous and fucking sweaty like I am. Then I just go for it and start to walk into them and it works sort of because they separate enough for me to squeeze by but not without bumping into them enough that they feel justified in punching me in the back as I pass.

They laugh when I wince as the pain runs through my spine like an electric fence crisscrossing my back. *–Fucking pussy–* they call out trying to get me to turn around but I don't. I push my way through the halls and listen to the angry names I'm called with each person I run into.

And I hate myself for not standing up to them. I hate myself for not turning around to smash my backpack into their fucking meaty faces even if it means getting a few bones broken in the afterward. But I can't. It's like everything inside me is paralyzed.

And that's why the demons love me.

I'm like a little boy who is afraid of the dark and they are the nighttime. I hate that little boy. I hate him more than anything else because it's his fault I'm the way I am. It's his fault that everything in my life sucks the way it does.

I push my way out of school and the fresh air begins to calm me down. The clouds have set in for the rest of the day. There is the smell of soap in the air that always comes before it rains.

I take quick short breaths to clear my mind.

I bury my feelings deep inside me.

I bury them where I have all the others buried . . all the memories that are hurtful . . all the things that knot me up inside if I think about them . . hoping that if I throw enough dirt on top of them then they won't come up anymore because they are not like flowers or plants that thrive in dirt . . they are corpses . . rotting.

—Think of something else. Think of something else— I repeat to myself as I walk toward the North Gym. Think of sports cars or bottle caps. Think of old television show reruns. Think of frozen pizza that needs to be put in the microwave. Think of sidewalks. Cash registers. Handwritten numbers. Anything so long as there are no feelings attached . . as long as they are numb and can numb me.

It works.

It always works.

And then I can be Dogboy again . . invisible to the demons again . . returned to the shadows. Safe until the next demon recognizes the little boy in my face . . and then I will have to go through it all over again.

By the time I see Sean and Keith standing near the sign

that tells passing cars the name of this terrible place I'm myself again. *–You ready?–* I say to them and they stop leaning against the letters that spell out Covington Senior High School and the three of us walk off to follow the path that runs alongside the road as the rain begins to fall drop by drop.

I don't mind the rain when I'm in the woods. I don't mind having to blow on my hands to warm them up or the water running down my face. None of that matters when I'm following the paths in the woods.

My whole life I've spent most of my time in the woods . . taking paths that turn their way through mazes of bark and bushes so thick that the world gets lost from view . . searching for the secret places . . the safe hiding places that every set of woods has tucked away somewhere.

I stay more than a few yards behind Sean and Keith.

–*Hurry up! Come on . . it's pouring!*– Sean calls out from up in front of me . . his voice swirling like the wind. I blow on my hands again and notice that it's much colder once the water has seeped into my clothes . . into my shoes so that my feet have gone numb.

It's hard to believe it's springtime. But I guess spring is

always a little like a baby that sometimes can't decide to cry or laugh. It never knows if it should feel like the end of winter or prepare us for summer.

I'm starting to get used to these woods. They no longer belong to strangers the way they did when I first stepped into them a month ago. They are beginning to become mine just like the woods back where my mom lives. The trees no longer look on me as an intruder. They let me pass without effort. They bury their roots to make it easier for my feet to find their way and curl through the crowded scenery. They accept me. They welcome me . . protect me.

When I catch up to Sean and Keith I can feel my face is glowing a soft pink color and my hands are raw and red from the cold.

The wind doesn't seem to bother them.

There is no color in their faces from the stinging cold.

I can just make out the spray-painted plywood that makes up the walls of our hideout. We have to be careful not to get our coats caught in the thorns that grow wild on either side of the narrow path that leads down to it. We have to be careful not to slip on the slick leaves that have been blown onto the ground though they are still fresh and green.

The path comes out into a clearing right in front of the door . . which is only another piece of plywood put on with one old hinge in the center and held closed with a padlock.

–Fucking hurry up with that– Keith says as Sean huddles over it . . his fingers slipping as he tries to perform the necessary combination that will take us out of the rain.

–Fuck off . . I am– Sean growls . . his fingers spinning the dial clockwise around and around and stopping . . counterclockwise once and stopping. *–And . . open sesame–* he whispers . . turning the dial clockwise again halfway and the lock slips open.

The smell of rotting leaves escapes into the air as Sean swings the door open. He takes a lighter from his pocket and I begin to make out the shape of the old bookshelf in the shadows. Keith pushes his way past us and I wait outside as he fumbles around in the dark.

It is like watching the sunrise as the shadows disappear.

Keith emerges with the old lantern burning brightly.

–Well don't be pussies . . fucking come in– he says . . how can we resist such a warm inviting welcome?

It may not look like much from the outside but there's plenty of room in the shack for us to spread out. Tree trunks have become seats. A series of boards taken from a house under construction have become a table. Nothing has become a floor though and the rain has run downhill under the walls and collects in little pools in the corners where it will wait for the heavier rains to come and help move it along into the creek that flows not too much farther along the path.

The whole place has the feel of a refugee camp.

The damp smell . . the thin walls that stand only with the help of each other. We are its refugees . . cast off . . finding home only when we are huddled into shacks way back in the woods and far from the roads and highways that everyone else calls home.

And it is the medicine that makes it feel like home to me.

The first taste of it is where I can start to relax.

Sean is busy preparing the first dose . . unrolling the plastic bag. The rotten stench of swamp water gives way to the smell of magic . . the smell of green crystals that melt in your mouth when the flame touches them and you breath in . . hold it . . hold it until your lungs hurt . . until the smoke becomes the blood through your veins . . and then let go.

–You got my lighter?– he asks Keith . . holding out his hand in nervous anticipation . . his other hand gripping the plastic soda bottle that has become a pipe half-filled with dirty water.

–I gave it back to you!– Keith says and I let my eyes pass from him back to Sean and my heart goes at circus speed hoping that when his hand dives into his pocket it will emerge with the tool we need in order to manufacture dreams.

–Oh yeah. I got it– he says and the three of us laugh in relief.

Quick whiff of butane as the spark catches. Sean's face seems to fade into the flames . . the shadows attaching themselves to the black of his clothing.

The weed burns like old newspaper in a fireplace . . slow at first . . then fiery like coal. *–yeah . . yeah–* Sean says as he draws the smoke in. *–yeah . . yeah–* drawn out like a slow-speed needle on a slow-speed record.

The smoke fills the room the way words in a novel fill my head.

Sean reaches over to hand everything over to me but I pass . . wave over to Keith even though I want so bad to take my turn next. But I don't. I'm patient. I've found the waiting makes all the difference.

Keith nods to me in appreciation . . takes a deep breath . . nods again as he exhales smoke like dragon fire on dragon tongue.

I didn't tell them that I'd never smoked before the first time the three of us did here. It didn't seem to matter if I'd ever gotten high before since I was going to get high then. Besides . . I didn't want all the attention on me . . didn't want them watching my every reaction to see if it was working the way my dad watches everything I do to see if maybe he can tell that I'm crazy.

I've only been to church once in my life. It was just after my mom left my dad and she went through a week of thinking that we needed *guidance.* She must not have found it though because we left quickly with her swearing under her breath about wasted time and stories full of bullshit.

I don't remember the stories but I remember the ceremonies.

Everything was so carefully set out like the set of a theater. The way the sun shone through the stained glass was like a spotlight so that the priest was backlit like an angel onstage. I was fascinated by how perfectly things were done . . how everyone knew exactly when to sit and when to kneel and when to say *amen* or start to sing.

It is the same way when the three of us sit around in a circle as the rain pounds the plywood. The drumming sound of the storm like the sound of psalms sung by a thousand voices.

There is a ritual to everything we do.

The pipe is handed to the next person in the right hand.

The lighter in the left.

Both items are received in the opposite hands.

All eyes watch the flame and everyone holds his breath except the person breathing fire medicine.

I feel it first in my ears. They feel clogged the way they do when I drive up the mountains. Then the feeling travels down like a dull heat to my eyes. It isn't until the cloud of smoke escapes me that my whole body begins to tingle like a million tiny fireflies are trapped under my skin.

–*Yeah* . . – I whisper.

Then we all look at each other with new eyes . . the sadness erased like mistakes corrected in my notebook. Not permanently erased. But it feels good to be mistake-free even temporarily.

–*Yeah*– I say again . . and I can feel my eyes closing slightly and for a brief second our laughter drowns out the thunder before I pass the lighter into Sean's right hand from my left.

–*Amen*– . . whispering to myself so they can't hear.

My dad has this thing about eating dinner together. He gets all worked up about it if one of us even suggests that we might be late or even worse miss it.

–Dinner hour is family hour– he says and then complains about the fall of our values. He mentions the stories on the evening news like a list of evidence. *–It all begins and ends at the table–* he says . . and my stepmom Janet nods her head in agreement.

I look at my watch.

I'm going to be late. At least fifteen minutes . . maybe more.

His lecture will start the way it always does . . with a stupid question like *–Do you know what time it is?–* I'll roll my eyes and mumble *–sorry–* and then he'll begin to talk about a piece he saw where a boy got in trouble with the law . . it is an unveiled warning to me . . an unveiled contempt for me too . . proof that he doesn't trust me . . that he suspects not everything with my mom was entirely her fault.

Today I can tell him it was the rain's fault.

It's not a complete lie. I've waited a little longer than I know I should have hoping the rain would slow. It only falls harder though.

–What's he going to do if you don't show?– Sean says to me when I tell them I have to go. I don't answer . . not really. I shrug my shoulders and repeat that I have to go.

–Pussy– Keith says . . but I don't let it get to me.

–Maybe– I say *–but I'm going anyway. I'll see you guys tomorrow.–* They just shake their heads and go back to looking through the stack of old pornos they've spent the last three years collecting and organizing in the shed like a well-kept library . . categorized by theme . . dog-eared to the best pages for quick reference.

I could have told them what I thought he might do.

I could have told them that I'm not sure he wanted me staying with him in the first place . . that he didn't exactly say he wanted me to come live with him and his new wife and new kid . . that what he really said was *–I don't want you staying there anymore–* when I called from my mom's trailer after Roy hit me the last time. I guess that maybe it's the same thing . . but somehow I can feel the differ-ence . . just a matter of a few different words but those few words are like a deep stomachache.

I could've told them but they would have said –*so what*– and that would have meant telling them about Roy and I don't think I could've done that.

–*Can I take one of those?*– I ask pointing to the magazines . . thinking one might come in handy if the rain continues to spill at a blinding pace.

–*Take this one . . it's fucking awesome*– Sean says . . closing the magazine in his hand and handing it to me neatly folded like a newspaper.

–*Nah . . I'm just going to use it as an umbrella*– I say.

–*Oh we know what you're gonna use it for*– Keith motions with his hand like he's jerking off.

–*Whatever*– I say. –*Just give me one you don't want anymore*– and Sean reaches into the box at his feet and tosses one at me . . commenting that I could use it as an umbrella or flush it down the toilet for all he cared.

–*Thanks.*– I pick it up off the floor as I leave.

The thing I've noticed about getting high is that it seems to fade away after a while but then when you change your surroundings it comes back as strong as the first few minutes. I had been thinking I was fine to go home when I was sitting in there . . when my eyes had dilated to the right size to take in the low burning light of the lantern. But then when I step outside it's like stepping back in time.

The last of the sunlight struggles for life behind the clouds . . behind the pine needles and oak leaves. Suddenly everything feels distant like an old home movie . . the world has turned into a coloring-book page painted in messy watercolor. The colors all running together in the rain.

I am ten minutes away from the road . . ten minutes into the trees and twenty minutes from the road to my dad's house. I'm going to be late . . really late.

I could run and get there quicker but my legs feel weak under the influence . . my eyes feel sore and worn out from studying naked pictures inside the low-lit shed.

So what? Let him yell at me. It's not like I haven't been yelled at my whole life. He can't even come close to yelling the way my mom or any of her drunken boyfriends can.

The magazine is turning soft in my hand . . the glossy paper begins to feel like oatmeal in the rain and I don't even think it's keeping me any drier than if I weren't using it. So I fold it up and put it under my jacket . . holding it close to my stomach in the waistline of my pants. Perhaps Keith is right and I will use it the way it was intended after all.

I'm trying not to focus my eyes on anything as I walk.

I'm trying to stay focused on walking. Because when I'm high I end up staring at things too long. I end up standing still and not even noticing it. So I don't let the clouds distract me . . I don't look up at them. I don't let myself pick out their strange gray shapes . . I don't look for castles the way Lacie taught me to do. I don't want to see them . . the strange crumbling palaces in the sky that float easily over the ocean . . floating as easily as Lacie's hand when she draws their soft shapes on paper.

It will only make me miss her.

So I walk without thinking. I walk with nothing on my mind except the next step in front me . . the next branch that I will have to duck . . the next snake hole that I will have to step over. I think about the road and how many dotted yellow lines I have to pass before I will be near enough to my dad's to see the warm yellow glow of electricity in the kitchen . . knowing that it's two steps for every line . . two steps in between them . . wondering if I can cut them in half to get there quicker.

I think I hear Sean and Keith erupt in laughter behind me.

I spin around and realize it's only thunder low to the ground.

I turn around again but my concentration is broken.

I start to look at things . . at the leaves that seem to grow in front of my eyes as they thirst on the rain . . at the raindrops that fall like ashes from a falling building.

Then the thunder booms again and I start walking.

–*It's only God bowling*– my mother used to say when I was little and scared. Then to make me laugh she would tell me that the rain was God pissing. I smile to myself even now . . remembering the sound of her voice as she said it.

But that was a long time ago . . that was when she was

still my mother . . that was before God starting pissing in bottles with warning labels on them.

I can see the road now. One car passes with its headlights like searchlights looking for deer to hunt . . the tires splashing water to the sides like a boat making a quick turn on a lake.

I'm ready to charge out in the traffic when a bird crosses the path. Not flying. Hopping. A hoppy bird with a long white neck and long orange legs. A lonely bird that doesn't mind the rain.

I move closer to it . . wondering if perhaps it wants to become my friend and I can be like Charlotte with her pig except I'd be a boy with his bird instead.

–*Tweet. Tweet-tweet*– trying my best to make a sound that sounds like it can fly. The bird looks at me . . studying me from head to toe . . but I guess I don't live up to its expectations of what a human friend should be because it lifts up its wings and flies away.

The dog begins to bark as I turn up the driveway. Any hope I had of sneaking in the bedroom window to get changed before they see me is gone.

Stupid dog.

He's supposed to be *my* dog. He's not supposed to bark when I come home . . maybe wag his tail a bit . . maybe whine softly in a tone that only I can hear. But he's not supposed to bark and give me away.

My dad bought him for me two years ago. He said it was to make me feel more at home when I came to visit. But that was the last time I visited him . . and now the dog is two years old and doesn't know me from any maniac who might come walking off the road.

I can see him . . front paws on the windowsill . . angry tooth snarl . . yelping to be released on me. *–Just give it some time–* my stepmom keeps saying. She says that about everything. She should make t-shirts . . TIME HEALS ALL WOUNDS . . sell them with a genuine smile because she believes that bullshit.

I'm not buying it though. That dog hates me.

My little half-sister comes to the window too. Pollyanna. I remember when she was born and my dad asked –*So how does it feel to be a big brother?*– and the only thing I could think of to say was that Pollyanna was the stupidest name I'd ever heard.

She is pointing . . hollering something over her shoulder like a proud tattletale kindergartner. Then she waves her hand excitedly like I'm a special visitor coming to her classroom.

I halfheartedly wave and halfheartedly smile.

She smiles and runs back toward the kitchen where I know my greeting isn't going to be as welcome.

I wipe my face clean with the rainwater . . hoping to wipe away the effects of the weed . . hoping to wipe away anything that might give away any emotions because I've been careful to hide everything I feel from my dad and Janet.

When I walk through the back door into the kitchen I'm blank . . like a white piece of paper without anything written on it . . like the last few pages in Lacie's sketchbook that haven't been given life by her pencil. I don't care what they read into it . . whatever they think has to be better than what I really feel.

–You're soaking wet!– Janet rushes over to the sink to grab a dish towel so I can dry my face and hands and the rain dripping from my hair.

The dog stops barking but he is eyeing me from the other side of the room . . watching for sudden movements . . distrustful the same as my dad.

Dinner is already on the table. The steam rises from under the lid on the dishes so I can't see what it is. But I can tell it's still hot . . so I must not be as late as I thought.

–What the hell were you out in the rain for?– my dad says.

–I don't know– I mumble.

–You never know anything . . do you?– he says and my stepmom gives him a look telling him to ease up. *–What?–* he says to her. *–It's true. He doesn't. That's all we ever hear from him . . I dunno–* and he droops his mouth and lowers his voice trying to imitate me but trying to make me look stupid and dumb with his mouth open.

I roll my eyes and shake my head.

–Whatever– I say. That always gets him . . turns his face red like hot glass . . curls his hand into a fist under the table until my stepmom gives him another look to remind him why I came here to stay in the first place. He unfolds his fingers slowly.

–Just make sure you don't track mud all over the floor– he says as I walk toward the bathroom to wash up.

36

I want to tell him I wouldn't have to be in the woods and track mud in if he didn't live out here in the sticks . . if he lived in the city like I thought he did . . like he said he did . . telling me he lived in Portland.

Portland my ass!

We live at least an hour outside of the city. Here is nothing like a city. Here the houses are all set far apart from each other . . set away from the road in wooded lots of land that don't give any protection. It's too lonely to keep the demons away . . too much open space for them to live in.

In the city the buildings rise up like concrete trees and the demons have more difficulty . . moving through concrete is not as easy as moving through soft soil.

In the city it's not as easy to pick me out among all the people filling the streets . . among the endless layers of windows atop windows . . in the sound of traffic . . a constant hum of machine music drowning out my voice which they follow like radar-driven parasites.

I never would have left Lacie for this. I was safer with her protecting me.

I only left for the city.

I left for its safe anonymity.

I probably shouldn't hate my dad for it though. I guess he really didn't know how much I wanted the city to be where I was. But still he shouldn't have lied to me . . shouldn't have said *Portland* when what he really meant was

Covington. And he shouldn't keep asking questions that he doesn't want the answers to. He doesn't want to understand me so I wish he'd stop getting annoyed when I don't try to explain myself.

–*What the hell are you doing in there?*– he shouts from the kitchen.

I turn off the faucet . . shout that I'll be there in a second. I hear the lids come off the dishes and the serving spoons scooping food onto the plates.

I throw my jacket into my room and stash the wet porno magazine under my bed before going back into the kitchen where they're all sitting around the table like a happy family in a television commercial . . so perfect and healthy and I'm like a stain on a new carpet.

My stepmom reaches for my plate and I hand it to her. –*Some of everything?*– she asks. I tell her *please* as she begins to shovel vegetables and potatoes and meat loaf onto my plate. My dad is still trying to avoid looking at me . . still trying to keep his anger to himself so Janet doesn't get mad at him for treating me bad.

Polly sits across from me . . staring at me the way she always does . . making faces as she pushes food into her mouth with her fingers. –*Isn't she a little old to be doing that?*– I said the first night I ate with them. My dad told me to leave her alone because she's only five . . I wanted to remind him how when I was five he refused to take us to a restaurant once because he was mad that I hadn't yet stopped sucking my thumb . . –*You're not a baby. You're FIVE years old for Christ's sake.*–

He's always been different with her. He's always picked her up and given her hugs where he would only touch me gently on the shoulder before pulling his hand away quickly.

Polly wrinkles her nose and I know that means she is going to ask a question . . I know from the way she's staring at me that it's another one of her questions about me. It seems there's one every night.

Why is Benji living here?

Is Benji really my brother?

Why does Benji get to stay up later than I do?

And my stepmom always gushes over them . . making that *oh-how-cute-is-she?* face that you see mothers making all the time in the mall.

–*She's just curious about you*– my stepmom tells me. And I wish she'd stop. It's not like I'm really even her brother. I'm just some stranger who is staying in their house until I'm old enough to get out. In two years I'll be gone and she'll forget everything about me so I wish she'd never try to learn.

–*Mommy?*– Polly says. Her eyes stay on me . . big and inquisitive and I know it's coming . . –*Why come Benji has hair like a girl?*–

My stepmom smiles.

Polly smiles.

They think it's so fucking cute.

Just like Roy. He thought it was cute too.

–*Shut up!*– I snap . . my fork jumping from my hand. Polly's eyes go dim and frightened.

The entire table jumps when my dad's fist slams down on the table. –*HEY! You don't tell her to shut up!*–

I refuse to look at him . . I refuse to let him see my eyes . . hide them behind my hair because I know they are showing too much . . I know my feelings are there on the surface and he doesn't understand and doesn't deserve to see them.

–*Cut your damn hair if you don't want her saying you look like a girl*– he says and goes back to eating.

I don't say anything as I get up from the table.

I don't answer him when he asks where I'm going.

I don't turn around when he calls my name as I head quickly to my room so that none of them can see me cry.

I hear Janet say –*Let him go . . it's okay*– as I close the door and shut the world out of my head.

Shadow of Yesterdays

The demons don't always show themselves.

Sometimes they hide behind the faces of people you know . . people you trust. Sometimes they hurt you over a long period of time . . hurting you with little things until the little things become so many that they strangle the air out of you when you try to breathe. Sometimes they strike fast . . a sweeping motion of the arm . . a closed fist leaving a bruise like a fashion on your face.

Sometimes they are strangers with slow hands.

The demons are the ones that make you hate yourself . . that let you know you are small and weak . . that they are stronger . . that they will always be stronger.

Roy is a demon.

The first time I saw him I could tell he was a demon.

Lips curling under his teeth like slugs hiding from the sun. Demon voice coming off of demon tongue. The feel

43

of hate in his hands. The shape of fire in his skeleton beneath his skin.

My mom isn't a demon. Demons just seem to find her easily. They attach themselves to her because she drinks and can't tell them apart from other people anymore. It is easy for them to get close to me through her. It is easy for them to fool her.

Roy fooled her.

He would come home with her late in the mornings. He would have to hold her up and help her through the tiny hallway of our trailer . . leave her in the bedroom to sleep until evening so that they could do it all over again the next night.

I never liked him being there.

I never liked the way he would sit around like he owned the place. *–Get me a drink!–* he would call out from the living room if I was in my bedroom. Sometimes it was *–Make me something to eat–* or *–Run your lazy ass to the store.–*

If I acted like I didn't hear him he would get off the couch and come over to my room . . bang on the door until I opened it then pull me out into the kitchen by my ear. *–Dammit I know you hear me you little shit–* he'd yell. Then he'd laugh and watch as I made him a drink or a sandwich. I'd try not to look at him.

–You'd make a good little maid– he'd say . . and I would feel my face burning with anger.

If I gave him a look he didn't like he'd hit me . . mostly in the side so that it wouldn't show . . but sometimes in the face and I'd feel my bones swell under the impact of his fist. *–That'll learn you to disrespect me–* as he shook the pain from his knuckles.

It was easy for a while just to stay away.

I would go to school in the morning before they got home and I would go to Lacie's afterward until they went out for the night. When he wasn't around I tried to talk my mom out of seeing him. And when she was sober she would agree. She would give me the same speech she always gave me about it being just her and me . . about cleaning up her act . . about how the two of us were a team and together we'd make everything okay again. *–We're the only survivors of this wreck–* she would say as she looked around at our home with its empty milk cartons and fast-food leftovers thrown about.

Everything would be okay for a day or two.

But then Roy would be over saying he was sorry for fighting with her . . he would say he was sorry to me . . sorry for the last time he hit me . . and for that night only he was sorry for anything she wanted him to be sorry for. At least until he was able to get her to a bar.

Everything got worse.

Mom's drinking got worse and worse so that I would never see her unless she was in her bedroom sleeping off the night before. When I did see her she barely knew who I was . . only knew that I was annoying the piss out of her with me trying to tell her what to do all the time.

She didn't want me around reminding her that once she used to be alive. She didn't want me getting in the way of her next bottle. It made her feel guilty just to look at me. –*Get OUT!*– she would scream whenever I would whisper something about her being a fucking mess or about Roy being a mean bastard.

She wanted me to leave and she wanted him to stay.

That is what demons do . . isolate the weak ones . . keep you away from anyone you might go telling to . . who might try to help you.

–*Looks like it didn't quite work out . . now did it?*– he said to me the day before he was supposed to move in.

–*What didn't?*– I asked . . trying not to look at him . . trying to concentrate on the television even if it was some old movie that I'd seen before and didn't even really like.

–*Your little plan to get rid of me.*– Taking another sip from the beer that I just got back from getting him.

I kept my eyes glued to the movie even as my heart began to jump inside me like a caged animal fighting its way through my ribs . . even though the back of my throat got all sore like when you know you did something that is going to get you in trouble and you're just waiting it out to see if they really know everything . . careful not to give away anything in case they don't know all that much.

–*Your mom told me about it. How you were calling me names and whining like a little brat trying to turn her against me.*– My body freezes up . . every muscle goes stiff and he can sense it. –*Yeah that's right. I know about it*– he said . . turning back to the television with his beer resting on his knee.

I should have left.

I should have walked out the front door and gone anywhere else. But it was late and it was cold and I thought maybe it would be better just to go to my room and let it all blow over. They'd be gone in a few hours anyway and I'd be at school before they got back.

But it's my fault.

I should have known better than to stay too near a demon when the demon had set its eyes on me.

I didn't really feel safe in my room . . even with the door locked and even with the headphones on to drown out the world. I could feel him in the other room . . could feel the demon inside him growing . . getting stronger . . madder.

I didn't care that maybe he was calling for me . . that

maybe he was knocking at my door. I turned the music up as loud as it could go and tried to disappear into the sad sound of the guitar singing to me.

When he broke open my door I heard.

When he yanked the headphones violently from my ears I could see that there was nothing but hate swimming behind the alcohol in his eyes.

It felt like a baseball bat swung into my sides when his elbow came down on my rib cage . . he cursed me . . *–I'm in damn charge here and you better start fucking listening when I call for you–* he said as he backed away from my bed trying to catch his breath from the quick explosion of anger.

I lay there covering my face with my arms . . curled up like a stupid little kid as he leaned against the wall laughing.

–Get up!– he said.

I didn't move.

–GET UP!– he commanded . . the threat of his fist visible. I uncovered my face and he laughed again when he saw my eyes were pink and swollen. *–Go on . . I ain't gonna hurt ya.–*

I knew it was a lie but I didn't know what else I could do . . so I straightened out my legs . . I bent over to sit up . . never taking my eyes off him . .

I never felt smaller than when I stood up as tall as I could and found it wasn't enough.

I never felt so fucking worthless as I did when he laughed . . when he pointed at me . . told me to pull my pants down. I didn't understand the words at first . . I didn't understand what he meant for me to do even though it was simple. *–Go on boy . . you heard me. Pull 'em down!–* and he knew I would because he knew I was weak and that he was strong and that he only had to raise his hand and I would flinch and do whatever he said.

He leaned against the wall as I undid the buttons . .

–All the way– he said with a motion of his hand as I stood there with my underwear around my knees.

I could feel the blood rushing to my head . . everything in front of me getting blurry the way it does before you pass out. The music was still playing in the headphones on the pillow . . like the sounds of another world where none of this was happening. I don't remember telling my hands to do it . . everything was automatic . . I wasn't alive anymore and my body was responding to commands like a computer while I tried to hide somewhere inside myself.

He made me stand there like a statue of a boy.

He made me turn around for him.

He made me walk toward him.

–Don't you look like a wimpy-ass little kid– he laughed.

I made myself go numb when he touched me . . it was only for a second . . only long enough to prove his point . . only until it was clear that I understood that I was nothing . . that there were new rules to follow and that I better not be getting any other ideas.

He left the door open as he walked out of my room.

He left me standing there so he could keep an eye on me and I don't remember moving for hours . . I don't remember going to sleep or getting up the next morning. I don't remember anything . . only the demon . . only the feeling of being a piece of shit.

I tear the pages out of my notebook that mention that night . . tear them into tiny pieces hoping that by doing so I can destroy the memories too . . that I can throw them out the window like snow falling from the sky and when they melt they will be no more.

But it doesn't work. It never works.

I always think about it.

Roy is always there standing in front me . . watching me . . laughing. And I am always the *wimpy-ass little kid* and it never changes no matter how many pieces of paper I can make out of my words.

I just have to think about something else.

ANYTHING ELSE.

Think about Christmas paper and presents . . think about stuffed animals like the ones in Polly's room . .

think about chairs and tables and the geometry of how they work together.

If I can only train myself to think differently then I can fix everything.

I don't tell anyone because if I don't tell anyone maybe it will be easier to forget it ever happened.

I didn't even tell Lacie.

I told her I was fine . . that everything was okay. Even when she cried when I told her I was moving I couldn't tell her the truth . . that I was going away to hide . . that here with my dad maybe I could hide from the past. I lied to her and told her it was my mom that I had to get away from.

It hurt when I lied to her.

But I couldn't tell her . . not when she is the only person who ever thought I was worth something. I didn't think I could handle the look on her face when she learned the truth . . that I was nothing.

Maybe here I can start to be a person again.

Maybe where no one knows me I can start over.

Meeting Strangers

She wears a black sweatshirt that's too big on her . . only her fingertips show beneath the long sleeves . . only the slightest slope of her shoulders seen under her hair that is like a tangled nest of damp straw drying slowly in the sun.

She wears jeans mostly and they are also a few sizes too big.

Her legs only show their shape when her knees bend.

The bottom of her jeans gets trampled beneath her sneakers and the white threads trail behind her like strange Native American jewelry.

But mostly it's her eyes that stand out . . green the way colors on the television are green . . artificially bright and electric.

Rianna Moore.

I saw her on my first day and knew that I wouldn't see

anyone prettier than her for as long as I went here. I thought for sure she was the most popular girl in school . . the way she walked through the middle of the hall while people moved out of her path . . moving her lips so slightly I knew she was singing to herself. I don't think anyone else notices because I don't think anyone else watches her the way I do.

–Why don't you go talk to her then instead of staring all the time?– Sean says to me. I hadn't known it was that obvious.

I've never seen her in this class before . . but usually I don't come to the library during study hall and I guess she doesn't usually have history class in the library either.

–Her?– I say . . pointing to Rianna and trying to play it off that I'm not that interested . . thinking Sean will find it uncool somehow that I'm into this girl who doesn't hang out with any of our friends . . who probably isn't into the same music as us . . who doesn't dress the way we do and isn't an outcast the way we are.

–Don't be an ass– he says . . I guess it is that obvious.

I don't know what I would say to her.

I would have said it already if I did.

–I know that other girl . . see her? . . that's her friend. I'll call her over here– Sean says. I want to tell him *no* so bad but at the same time I want him to.

–CAM!– Sean yells . . and it seems to me that the entire library turns around while I try to hide my face. He waves

56

her over with a violent motion of his hand. *–Come here a second–* he shouts as she wrinkles her eyebrows not really wanting to . . then she says something quick to the girl she is with and walks toward us like she's afraid of us . . like she doesn't appreciate being summoned by the two freaks at the back table.

I look up at the clock on the wall hoping that time will move faster . . hoping that it will move on to next period before Sean has a chance to say anything to this girl.

Cam refuses to get too near us. She stands a few feet away from the table where Sean has a magazine open in front of him and I have my notebook with a pretty bad sketch of Rianna in it.

I turn the page and cross my fingers hoping Cam didn't see it.

–What?– she asks . . impatiently tapping her foot.

–You're friends with Rianna Moore . . right?– he asks. She nods and glances back over her shoulder where her friends watch cautiously. *–Well my friend Dogboy here is drooling all over about her . . think you can help him?–*

–Fuck off– I say under my breath and look down at my hands to hide my face because it's burning red.

–Really!– Cam says and her eyes grow wide . . magnified by her thick glasses . . excited . . and she moves in closer to our table and pulls out a chair because she feels safer knowing that Sean has called her over to gossip.

I think about denying it . . telling this girl Sean made it all up and send her on her way.

–*You're the new kid . . right?*– she says to me.

Sean picks up his magazine and returns to his normal state of slow-motion disinterest.

–*Um . . yeah . . I guess*– I stutter and Cam smiles.

–*Your name's* Dogboy?– making a face like it is something she is allergic to.

–*Benji really*– I say . . and Sean begins barking and howling until I elbow him in the side and he laughs. –*But everyone calls me Dogboy*– and that makes Cam laugh.

–*I think it's kinda cute*– she says. If it wasn't for Rianna and the promise of finally hearing the sound of her voice I would tell this Cam girl to fucking get lost.

–*Maybe . . it's just a name*– deciding on the calmer reaction that doesn't involve offending her.

–*So you like Rianna?*– and I feel like telling her we're not in fifth grade and therefore can we not use words like *like* because I don't even know her . . only what I've seen . . only the things I can observe . . things like black being her favorite color or that she dots her letters with little hearts instead of dots and I have no idea why that doesn't make me sick to my stomach like it would if I saw any other girl do it.

I shrug my shoulders.

–She doesn't have a boyfriend– Cam says and winks at me once *–hint hint–* so I want to punch her in the face except for the fact that she just told me the one piece of information that I've been after for the past week.

I allow myself to smile but only enough for me to know.

–Do you have a girlfriend?– she asks . . making herself go all shy the way girls do when they ask questions like that . . like they're flirting with you for someone else just to see how well you do it.

Lacie.

I can see her in my mind . . how she was the first time we met each other from a distance . . her waving at me from across the lunchroom and turning bright red and how it made me on fire inside to watch her.

But that seems so long ago . . so far away.

Is she my girlfriend still?

Can she be if she's living in another life . . if she's living in a life that I left behind me?

She was always more than my *girlfriend* . . she was the angel who protected me. But angels can't keep you safe when they are not near enough to touch.

–You do . . don't you?– Cam says.

I tell her *–Sort of.–*

I feel guilty about the *sort of* even as the words are leaving my lips.

59

–Doesn't matter– she says *–I won't tell if you won't–* and another wink and even though I was the one who made it sound unimportant I still hate her for saying it *doesn't matter* because what does she know about anything . . what does she know about Lacie and how much she means to me and that if I could help it I would make myself forget about Rianna and convince myself that she's the ugliest girl I've ever seen.

–Excuse me Miss Chase– and I look up to see Cam's teacher hovering around our table like a demented bird . . *–This time is for you to work on your research paper* not *to talk to your friends.–* And then he walks two steps away but waits there to make sure the conversation comes to a quick end.

–Gotta go– she says and frowns . . promises to tell Rianna all about me though she knows nothing about me. *–See ya Sean–* waving her hand between his face and the magazine. He mumbles something as she leaves.

I can see all her friends waiting for her to get back . . dying to know what the hell she was talking to us about . . and then she looks back and points and I put my head down again because I don't want to see the look on their faces . . I don't want to be the center of their attention.

I open my notebook and try to think of something to write . . anything . . but the only thing I can think about is how I hope Cam doesn't say anything to Rianna before last period . . how much I'm dreading the moment I see her look at me and know that she knows and worry so hard about what she might think.

But at the same time I want Rianna to know this second . . because I want to know her reaction.

I run through the halls to be the first one into class . . running like my life depends on getting there before Rianna does . . pushing past angry girls telling me –*Watch it.*–

No one is in the room when I sprint through the door trying to catch my breath.

I'm overwhelmed by the smell of chalk and desks and more than a little light-headed so that the rows seem to move the way boats rock when they are out on the ocean.

I decide to sit far away from the windows.

I want to sit as far from where she will be as possible.

I'm terrified of seeing Rianna look at me like I'm some kind of complete nightmare.

I should have stopped Sean.

Because I hate feeling this way . . I hate feeling scared.

One by one the other kids in my class come in . . fill in

the areas around me like a wall going up around a city. I only wish I felt as protected as all of that.

I don't look at anybody and hold my hand under my shirt trying to stop my heart from beating so fast . . trying to apply pressure like you do with wounds . . trying to make it stop completely.

But then Rianna walks in and I remember for an instant what it's like to be alive and how sometimes even when life feels at its worst it can still feel so incredible at moments that it almost makes up for everything that is horrible in the world.

I watch her with my head down . . hair hanging in front of my face . . watching her keeping her head still . . never turning to look at me . . looking only near the windows where she always sits.

I wonder if she knows . . does she know she is being watched and is she walking more carefully . . or is she trying to be even more beautiful only for me?

It's pretty to think of anyway . . it's comforting to imagine.

She takes the window seat nearest the front. She pushes her hair away from her face and tucks it behind her ear and turns to the side so I can see her face . . the small slope of her nose . . the perfect shape of her natural strawberry-pink lips.

I see her look over her shoulder . . scanning the row next to her . . the row next to that . . then she looks farther out and when she sees me her eyes stop and I can feel my bones turn to glass.

Then she smiles quickly and quickly turns away.

I try to convince myself that I didn't see it . . that I made it all up . . that maybe she didn't smile at all and maybe it was only the beginning of a sneeze.

My mom always used to tell me —*You're never satisfied*— because I would never let myself get too excited when she got me exactly what I wanted most in the world for my birthday or Christmas because I didn't want to believe it was true at first just in case I was only daydreaming . . because if I never build up hope then I can never be disappointed or hurt.

I don't pay attention to anything in class except her for the whole period.

I watch every little move she makes . . the way she turns her wrist . . the way she rests her mouth on her hand the way kittens do when they lick their paws to clean themselves.

She doesn't look at me again.

She doesn't even glance over to her right even once in the entire forty-two minutes and I'm convinced it was all my imagination . . I hate myself for letting myself believe even for a little bit that her smile was meant for me.

Thursday 2:51 pm

I have my books packed up five minutes before the bell rings . . I have my feet ready to go three minutes before. I start standing up as the second hand passes the nine on the big clock over my head. I am at the door as the first sounds are being heard throughout the school.

Fresh air is the only thing on my mind.

I couldn't breathe in the classroom . . the air tasted hot and the sweat formed little beads at first on my forehead . . then on my back . . then running in streams down my skin and I was being strangled slowly by everything in the room . . by the desks . . by the teacher's voice like a vise gripped around my neck and squeezing tighter with each sound he made.

I stumble to the exit where the sun shines through the doors the way light always shows through heaven in the movies.

I feel the way a baby must feel taking its first breath after being born . . the air in my lungs. I lean against the outside wall of the school and let myself slide down to the ground . . slipping in slow motion.

The rush follows after me.

Thousands of sneakers filing out the door . . spreading out over the concrete . . spreading away from me as they make their way toward buses or cars or wherever else they may be going after school. I'm supposed to be following them too . . supposed to meet Sean . . supposed to cloud my mind with smoke that will make me forget the burning feelings inside me that I endured for the past forty minutes like a short visit into hell.

But I don't feel like it today.

I feel like sitting here until everyone has passed.

I feel like watching the sun set out beyond the trees.

I feel like waiting under the stars until morning.

I feel like staying still until someone comes along to ask if I'm dead or alive because maybe then I will know the answer.

But that all ends the moment I see her walk out . . her jeans being ripped under shoes as they scrape against the cement . . shuffling along slower than the rest and I want to crawl around the corner to hide.

Then she sees me and it's too late.

–*Hey*– she says. There is nothing behind me but a brick

wall and no one to the side of me so I can't pretend I think she's talking to someone else. I hold my hand up to wave but put it down fast and maybe she will be annoyed and decide not to bother with me.

She approaches me the way she would a stray dog . . cautious . . wondering if I will bite if she tries to pet me.

–What're you doing?– she asks.

I feel choked inside but there is something about her voice that makes me fight through it . . like a song that begs you to sing along to it even if you are embarrassed by the way you sing . . even if strangers are listening . . even if you don't know the words.

–I don't know . . waiting I guess– I say.

–For what?–

–Anything really . . tomorrow . . tonight . . I don't know. Just waiting.– And I think she is going to say *oh* and start to walk away.

–Mind if I wait with you?– she says and doesn't wait for me to answer . . just sits down next to me on the cement with her legs folded together and begins to play with the white threads that hang loose from the bottom of her jeans.

I know I'm supposed to say something but I can't think of anything. I've always been terrible at this. I've always made girls think I'm weird because I go so silent when it's only me and them.

My friend Avery never had that problem. He knew what to say at every moment . . knew how to say it so that girls would flutter their eyes and make soft sounds with their tongues. I always hated him for it . . I always hated that he made it look so easy.

–*Rianna . . right?*– is all I can think of . . trying to sound like I don't know who she is . . trying to make her believe that maybe I never even talked to her friend Cam.

–*Yeah*– she says with a little nod of her head. The sun goes behind a cloud and I can see her clearly . . and she is real in my life for the first time which makes me smile . . but I'm careful not to let her see it. –*Where're you from?*–

–*It's a small town . . you wouldn't have heard of it*– I tell her . . and she says maybe she knows it anyway.

I say the name of my mom's town and Rianna tells me –*You're right . . I've never heard of it.*– And I laugh for the first time that I can remember in such a long time that hasn't been forced or faked. I cut it off because it startles me.

–*You like it here?*– she asks . . turning back to the sun but not enough to keep me from being able to see the corner of her smile . . smiling more at the glare of the sun than at me but it doesn't seem to matter either way . . either way it seems to make me feel safe.

–*I guess . . not really*– I say and reach over beside me

where a weed is growing through the cracks in the side-walk . . feeling the tiny hair thorns as I snap it off at the stem and feel the green color rubbing off on my hands.

–Yeah. It's not so great . . is it?– she says.

I nod to agree but suddenly it doesn't seem so bad.

She's wearing a perfume that every girl I ever knew in middle school wore . . faint scent of mosquito spray and vanilla.

I toss the weed from my hands. Her head turns to watch it fall.

I watch her and wonder if she would run if I kissed her.

–You wanna walk with me to the gym?– she asks.

I must look as confused as I feel because she smiles and explains that she has to go to training . . that she has Junior Nationals in the fall. When I ask her for what it's her turn to laugh. She tells me *–gymnastics–* and says that she thought I knew because she forgets sometimes that not everybody knows.

–Oh . . I'm sorry– I say because I feel guilty although I'm not sure why.

–No . . it's okay. It's just sometimes I forget that I'm not only a gymnast. Usually that's all people know about me.–

And I nod because I think I know what she means. I know what it's like to be thought of as only one thing and nothing else . . know that no matter what you do you are only what other people see you as. I want so bad to tell her that I know but not yet . . not right this second because it's sort of like she knows . . the way she picks up the weed I tossed and twists it once around her finger before putting it in the front pocket of her backpack where the zipper is broken.

I stand up after her . . pick up my bag as she brushes the dust from the back of her black sweatshirt . . asking me if there are any marks on her. I tell her no.

We walk two feet apart from each other.

We both stare at our feet and only look up to watch a bird that flies by in front of us.

–*My name's Benji*– I say quietly when we get closer to the gym.

–*Huh?*–

–*My name's Benji.*–

–*I know*– she says and walks a few feet in front of me.

The door to the gym is open . . people are moving back and forth laying down mats and pulling different types of equipment into place . . balance beam . . vaults. The powder from their hands swirls like a dust storm.

–*Will you walk me again tomorrow?*– she asks . . but she doesn't wait for me to answer as she takes two fast steps into the gym. Then she turns around long enough to see me nod and she smiles so that her freckles disappear.

I wait for her to go into the locker room . . watching

until the door closes behind her and she is gone. Then I start to walk away from the school building . . heading to the woods . . but I won't go to meet Sean and Keith . . not today. I will just take the shortcut back to my dad's house where I will wait for tomorrow.

Hunting the Prey

The rain is falling so loud outside that it woke up my little sister. I hear her scream after every explosion of thunder and try to figure out which sound is the one that woke me up.

Both seem powerful enough to keep me awake . . to keep me away from the dogs that chase me in my dreams.

The dogs fade as my eyes adjust to the darkness.

My dream is like things painted on old yellowing paper and the shadows spill across them like black ink . . pulling me back to my real body.

In my dream I'm able to run the way rabbits run . . fast on four legs and pushing through the tall grass that grows so thick together it is like swimming as I run.

I'm always me in my dream . . but I'm always the brown rabbit too. The scent of a rabbit on my skin is why the dogs chase me.

The shadows in my bedroom disappear in a sudden burst of electric sky . . making my eyes white like the color of lightning.

I count the spaces between the flash and the thunder the way my grandmother taught me to when I was little. I know something is about to happen.

One one-thousand.

Two one-thousand.

Three.

–*MOMMY!*–

The thunder is closer than last time and Polly's screaming is louder than last time too.

I listen to the sound of her bare feet running through the hall . . running like I run in my dreams.

She opens and closes the door to my dad's room as the next spark leaves its impression burned on the sky.

The rain comes hard after the thunder . . a million pieces of clouds falling down wet to the window where I can see the trees waving their branches as they hold tight into the ground with their roots . . and I wonder why they never let go . . never let themselves get taken up by the storm and spread their leaves far over the ground.

I would.

I'd let the storm catch me the way I always let the dogs catch me before I wake up . . dogs with angry teeth . . with fiery manes . . fire trailing behind them as they hunt me.

I am always standing in the grass when they come for me . . always surprised how flat the land is . . the field stretching out to the horizon with nothing to break up the evenness . . always surprised how quickly the dogs approach me when they seem so far away at first and don't seem to move so fast.

I run too late and they are always so close . . their hot breath on my back and growling the way thunder growls through the sky.

I try to make quick turns . . darting left and right and kicking up dirt as I move . . springing from my hind legs like arrows fired from bows strung so tight they barely keep from snapping.

There is no place to hide once I start to run . . no holes to dip into . . no trees to climb . . and I can feel my energy giving way as they get closer.

It's not so much that I let them catch me as it is that I simply stop running when I come to a stream that divides the world in half. It's narrow . . not so wide that I couldn't jump it or swim across . . but the sight of the other rabbit children drowning there scares me and I can no longer think of getting away.

I can smell the smoke from where the ground has turned to ash on each spot the dogs have passed over . . the dry grass catching on the sparks trailing behind them and the sky turning orange the way nuclear explosions turn the sky orange . . the way they turn clouds to vapor like gasoline fumes.

I know when they have reached me. I don't need to turn around . . their hungry faces perfectly reflected in the swollen eyes of the other rabbit children whose drowned bodies drift downstream.

I can either join them or wait for the dogs to tear my body to pieces. Either way there will be a moment or two of pain . . either way I won't stop feeling fear until I'm dead.

I never know which I choose because I always wake up right when I have to decide.

I used to tell Lacie about my dream . . tell her how I didn't know which was better. She would frown as she ran her fingers through my hair.

–*Neither*– she would say when I would ask which she would choose. –*You should make up a new ending*– she said . . and then told me about the castle in the clouds where the princess of the sky lived . . told me that I should grow wings and fly there so I could meet her and everything would be okay. I told her it was pretty to think of it like that but inside I'm not so sure it works that way.

I get up from my bed and try not to think about dogs and clouds and dreams because maybe it all means that I have to wait until I'm dead before I feel safe . . and I don't want to think that way.

I want to think that I can be happy . . that if I can just

78

find the right place to hide or run with more speed . . if I can find the courage to jump over the river and leave the painful things behind me . . maybe then I can be okay but it's too hard to think about sometimes.

Sometimes it's better just to watch the rain outside.

Sometimes it's better not to think too hard.

–Benji . . you'll be late for school!– Janet shouts through my bedroom door as she passes by on her way to the kitchen.

I'm already ready.

I won't be late for anything.

I want to tell her to mind her own business . . that no one has had to take care of me for years and that I don't need her to start. But I figure that would only lead to a new argument with my dad about *gratitude* and *manners* so I let it go . . finish throwing my books in my bag and throw it over my shoulder.

I didn't think I'd miss much of anything about my mom's house or her routine when I left but I sort of do miss the times when no one was around. I miss the solitude of the mornings . . waking up in an empty house and getting myself together without anyone disturbing me with concern.

It's not like that here. It's never empty . . especially in the morning.

My dad and Janet have their schedules worked out so that they can be home with Polly before school . . how cute for her and inconvenient for me.

I try to go unnoticed through the kitchen . . keeping my head down . . stepping softly . . holding my breath.

–Can I fix you something to eat?–

I have no idea how she even knows I'm here . . her back turned . . the cartoons blasting from the other room while Polly sings along to the theme song.

–Um . . no thanks– I say.

–You have to eat something . . you can't go all morning without eating– she says. I want to explain to her that my need to be alone is greater than my need for food but she already has a bowl out and three boxes of cereal.

–I have to go . . I'm gonna be late remember– and she smiles at me in a way to let me know that I'm being a smart-ass.

–I'll get the milk– she tells me . . and I guess I have no choice but to put my bag down and take a seat where the dog is already waiting for me because he's my best friend when there's food nearby. I pour some sugar flakes into my hand

and let him lick them from my palm. He walks away a few steps to eat them just in case I decide to take them back.

My stepmom shouts into the other room for Polly . . telling her it's time to eat and that she'll have to turn the television off. *—I'm not going to tell you again young lady—* she says even though I've heard her tell Polly at least four times already this morning.

My dad comes in the room first . . he is dressed for work . . shaved . . hair brushed back so I can see where his hairline is reaching farther back on his forehead. *—Aren't you going to be late?—* he says when he sees me pouring milk into my bowl.

I throw my arms out to my side . . what the fuck does he want . . I didn't want to stay anyway.

But Janet steps in before he can get too angry at me for slamming my spoon down on the table . . touches him lightly on the chest and whispers that it's okay . . that she told me to eat something first.

My dad doesn't apologize . . not that I expected him to . . not that he ever has . . but still it would've been nice to at least pretend he was sorry for accusing me.

Polly comes up behind him . . shuffling her bare feet along the tile . . arms folded in front of her and her face all pouty. I can't help but smile at her misery . . at the fact that maybe she is more like me than I give her credit.

—I hope you know that show is my FAVORITE SHOW

EVER!– she announces and my stepmom just smiles and says it will be on again tomorrow. *–Well it's still not fair–* Polly says . . stomps her foot down and mopes over to the table.

The dog goes over to her then . . puts his snout on her lap begging for some of her breakfast too. She pushes him away and my dad looks up at her. *–That's enough–* he says. She frowns . . pushes the hair away from her face but doesn't carry on anymore . . sits up straight and points to the type of cereal she wants.

I'm finishing as quickly as I can . . planning my escape . . hoping to get out before anyone has time to notice me enough to ask me anything.

–So Benji . . – my dad says.

Too late.

I took one too many bites and now I know it's coming . . I know from the look on his face that he has something on his mind . . something he's been planning.

–Yeah?–

–Are you . . um . . going to tryouts today?– and I hate how he does that . . says something like I'm supposed to know what the hell he's talking about . . like it's not coming out of nowhere which it is.

–For what?– I ask.

–Aren't the baseball team tryouts today? I thought I saw it in the school newsletter.–

What is he asking me for? I couldn't care if it's today tomorrow or never.

I shrug to let him know how much I care and he tells me that he's pretty sure they are today.

–So?– I don't mean it to be mean but he gives me that look that tells me it is . . that I'm giving him attitude.
–Dad . . I haven't played baseball since I was eight years old.–

I never liked it then either.

I sucked.

I hit the ball once in three years.

I hated it.

I hated the way he loved it and I hated more the way he would tell me every player is important . . even the ones who suck.

–You'll never know unless you try– he says now and looks at his newspaper.

I want to ask him if he is crazy . . if he woke up this morning and completely lost his mind. Doesn't he remember how I would cry before practice . . how I would beg him to let me stay home and how angry he would get at me . . how he would lecture me about teamwork?

–No. I do know. I hate it– I say . . because I'm not eight years old anymore and I'm not going to sit here and listen to him tell me that I might like something that I absolutely do not.

His fist comes down hard and sudden on the table.

The silverware and bowls jump and Polly looks startled as milk spills from her bowl and onto her nightgown.

–Dammit! I'm not going to watch you sit around here all the time with that Sean boy doing nothing!–

I can feel the anger rising up my spine . . my voice growing inside me the way a roar grows over time and I'm ready to explode when Janet steps in . . holding her hand out to me . . gesturing for me to calm down . . gesturing for him to calm down . . giving him a look to let him know he's going too far as she wipes Polly's nightgown with a napkin.

–Don't give me that look Janet– he says . . then turns back to me. *–I'm not your mother!–* he says *–I'm not going to let you waste your life just because she was willing to.–*

–I'm not wasting ANYTHING!– I shout . . jumping up from my chair as he tells me not to yell. I want to do more than that . . I want to tear apart the whole goddamn room . . throw dishes against the wall so that they shatter as I scream to cover the sound. I want to flip the table over . . I want to do anything that will make him notice that I'm not what HE wants me to be . . that I'm me . . right here . . open your fucking eyes Dad and look at me!

–All I ask is that you think about it– he says . . calmer . . the old settle-down trick.

–Whatever– I say and grab my bag and head for the door.

School should be optional. I shouldn't have to go if on certain days the thought of it exhausts me. I'm not going to get anything out of it. I'll be pissed off all day and probably only end up getting in trouble anyway so why not just skip it altogether and save everyone some time.

My mother always seemed to agree.

I never had to go to school if I didn't feel like it. As long as I passed my classes she figured what's the difference. –*You're getting enough school if you pass*– is what she would say and that was just fine with me.

I don't get the impression that my dad and I are going to see eye to eye on that one either.

The halls are filled with voices on top of voices . . conversation running into conversation and becoming one constant hum like the irritating sound of highways. I'm not in the mood to focus on any of them so I block them out . . barrel through on my way to homeroom without looking for any of my friends to talk to.

It has nothing to do with them . . just that my dad makes me so fucking crazy.

I know what he's trying to do. I know he doesn't give a shit about me playing baseball . . that it has nothing to do with baseball at all. I wish he'd just come out and say what he means. That was always the thing about my mother . . she might throw things and scream but at least that was something I could understand.

My dad always tries to talk around things.

But I see through that . . I know what he really meant this morning . . I know it has nothing to do with me sitting around but has everything to do with Sean and how he sees us both as freaks.

He's always wanting to change me.

He's worried about how I'll *end up.* He's scared I'll be like the kids in the city.

But what's so wrong with them? At least they're real people . . at least they're not faking to be happy in their little fucking homes where people pretend there are no such things as demons that destroy your life from the inside out.

If he cared that much about me where the hell was he when my mom would come home early in the morning with some new asshole helping her stand up . . helping themselves to everything she had including me?

He doesn't have any right to try to fix me.

FUCK HIM.

Fuck everyone.

I don't need any of them . . I don't need anything.

I'll run away to the city and live on the streets just to show him that I don't care what he thinks. Let him drive by me in his car. He won't even recognize my dirty face when I give him the finger.

I'll be safe.

I'll live in the shadows.

I don't need his happy family. It's not like I can blink my eyes and pretend the last seven years of my life never happened . . –Hi daddy I'm home. Practice went great today– . . no . . that's Polly's life not mine . . he didn't want to give it to me before . . I'm sure as hell not going to accept it now.

I walk straight for the door . . numb from the noise . . dizzy from all the people walking past me . . pushing me left or right . . in and out of focus.

I only care about getting out of here.

I don't see Sean until he grabs me by the arm and nearly pulls me to the ground because I'm walking so fast away from everything. He has a wool hat pulled down over his eyes and I don't recognize him . . my hands already made into fists as I was walking and it's just a reaction when I pull my arm back ready to punch him in the face.

–Hey hey . . what the hell are you doing?– and his voice I know but my eyes are burning and then slowly his face becomes clear.

–Ah . . hey . . Sean– shaking my head . . fever vision and sweat on my forehead. *–I . . um–* and he tells me I don't look so good.

I tell him I don't feel so good either and he tells me that's because I need a cigarette. I can't imagine that's true but it sounds as good as anything else.

–Sure– and we head outside where it smells green like new grass and gray like the wind. We just have to go across the road to the other side where it is no longer school property.

It feels good to be away from the commotion inside the school. It's like my brain is filtering things down to one thing at a time . . like if I had been watching ten movies and one by one they turn off so that there is only one screen calling for my attention.

–Here– Sean says.

My hands are shaking when I go to take the cigarette from him. I blow on them but they're not cold . . I'm not shivering . . fucking worked up is all.

I hold my hair away from my face as the flame touches paper and turns my breath to smoke.

–Better?– Sean asks. I don't know how or why but I realize that it is better.

–*Sorry*– I say . . not really sure what I'm sorry about . . maybe for almost beating him up . . maybe for being so jumpy like I am in my dreams when I have rabbit legs. –*My dad . . you know . . pisses me off sometimes*– and Sean waves the smoke away from his eyes and tells me not to worry about it.

I look over at our school . . see kids dipping in and out of view in the windows . . not really able to hear the roar of their voices but still able to sense them. I think if I go back in there they will destroy me . . like some new weapon the demons have come up with . . sonic assault.

It has the look of a prison from outside . . strong brick walls that no huffing or puffing could blow down . . metal strips crisscrossing the windows like bars disguised as architecture. No one cares about anything in there except keeping us inside.

–*Let's get out of here*– I say.

Sean laughs . . his breath coming from his nostrils like a bull. –*Go where?*– he says.

–*I don't care.*– I'm ready to go to the other side of the world if that's what it takes to leave all of this behind me.

–*I've got enough trouble*– he says and drops his cigarette under his foot where the fire leaves black marks on the dirt. He takes a step onto the road . . looking both ways before crossing . . looking back to me . . –*You coming?*–

I take a deep breath . . notice that my hands are no longer shaking.

–I guess I am– I whisper because I know I'm not brave enough to go alone. Sometimes the thought of it is enough though . . enough to get me through another day.

I don't want to wait for her with everyone else around.

I don't know if she wants anyone to know about me because our time is like a secret that we keep between each other. It's only a little bit of time . . the small space between when school ends and the rest of the world begins . . but it's ours . . it's private.

I wait for that part of the day from the very beginning.

Today is even worse because I don't want to be here in the first place. But the second I see her it seems right that I stayed.

I like to watch her walk outside and stop to look for me. Time runs so slowly then . . everything so perfect then for a few seconds that I don't care about anything in the world except her.

I'm going to ask her maybe to hang out this weekend.

If she says yes I will stay here. I will stay in Covington

because she is here. It won't matter if my dad pisses me off or if school pisses me off . . as long as I have something . . one thing in my life that doesn't suck.

–*Hi Benji*– she says. I come away from the wall to meet her the way actors meet actresses onstage . . the sun a full spotlight . . the sounds of the fields in the near distance like the soundtrack to divide us from everyone else.

–*Hey.*–

I feel like a skeleton standing next to her . . more bones than skin. I'm afraid to touch her . . afraid my hands will cut her with their sharp edges.

We walk past the large windows of the library . . our reflections distorted like they're in carnival mirrors as we step with the exact same timing of our feet . . me taking smaller steps than normal to keep in rhythm.

She waves to people who pass us . . people I don't know . . people who wouldn't notice me except that I'm with her. I turn away and look out toward the trees and the cars pulling away from the parking lot so that I don't have to see what they think about me.

I see Rianna pull her hands into her sleeves . . only the tips of her fingers poke out and I want so bad only to hold her hand . . to know if it is cold the way Lacie's always were.

–*Rianna?*– I say as we get near the gym . . as we get nearer to saying good-bye for the weekend. I have to ask her . . the butterflies in my stomach want me to stop . . want me to let it pass . . to stay silent and hope for the best. But I don't want to spend the entire two days wondering if next week she will want to forget about me and find someone new to walk with her after last period.

She doesn't say anything . . only looks at me . . her freckles showing clearly in the sun . . the purple color of sleep around her eyes.

–Do you . . um . . do you wanna hang out tomorrow?– and I have to put my hands in my pockets to hide them from shaking in front of her as my voice cracks on each syllable.

–I can't– she says . . and I knew it was too good to be true . . knew that nothing in my life was ever meant to work.

I pretend that my heart is still in one piece when I tell her it's okay . . and that's when she touches my wrist above where my hands are sunk deep into my jeans.

Her hand is warm like coal.

–I have practice– she says . . still holding my wrist . . tugging on it gently until I pull my hand out of my pocket and her palm presses flat against my palm as the clouds eclipse the sunlight.

–Does that mean you would if you didn't?– I ask. She only smiles and lets go of my hand.

She begins to walk as I stand there . . *–Aren't you coming?–* she says and walks faster so that I have to hurry to catch up to her just as she is about to go into the gym.

–Sundays I only have a half day of practice– she says.
–You can come over in the afternoon.–

I know I wouldn't be able to speak if I tried so I stay quiet and let her scribble her phone number down on an old quiz where she got two questions wrong out of ten . . she doesn't seem to care if I know which questions she didn't understand.

She tells me to call her on Saturday after dinner.

–Okay– I whisper as she hands me the paper. I fold it carefully in half so that it can fit in my notebook without getting wrinkled at all because I know this piece of paper could possibly save my life.

–So call me tomorrow . . okay?–

I nod as she goes inside . . nodding as the gym door closes and the last bus pulls away. I'm too stunned to follow them out.

Before I got on the bus to come live with my dad Lacie promised that she would always be there looking over me . . she said the girl who lived in the clouds would protect me.

I touched her face and kissed her and said –*sure she will*– even though I didn't believe in the power of angels the way I believe in the power of demons.

I believe in angels now though.

I believe in them when I close my eyes because I can still see Rianna's face like a photograph pasted over the darkness. I can still feel the touch of her hand on my hand when I squeeze it so tightly into a fist . . her scent of bug spray and vanilla on my clothes.

I reach over the side of my bed to get my notebook.

Her phone number is there . . written on her algebra quiz. Looking at it I feel the way I do when I read the fortune inside a cookie . . the numbers full of promises that may or may not come true.

I study her handwriting . . trace the heart shape of the *i* in her name. I solve the two problems that she got wrong and write the correct answers next to the ones she wrote down and wonder if that means together we're perfect.

I can see the clouds outside my window from where I lie down on my bed . . way up high in the sky and waiting for the night to come . . holding off as long as they can . . holding off until summer when they can stay longer and longer every day.

That is where the angels live.

I look at the words that I've written in my notebook. The blue ink on white paper looks a little like the sky . . with more words it would look like the sky outside my window.

I write about Rianna living up there. I pretend she lives there to watch me way down below where I am a rabbit child and she is an angel that doesn't need wings to fly.

That is where the angels live.
Sunlight is the color of her skin.
She watches over me.
Demon fire not far away.
Her shadow on my rabbit head.

I study all the words . . the careful way in which I wrote each letter on each line.

It sounds good to read them aloud . . a safe rhythm . . a pretty picture.

I don't write about the end . . I don't write down that she sends the demons away.

I don't write about those things because I don't want to get caught up in happy endings.

I close my notebook.

I close my eyes.

I try to believe in happy endings.

Sunday Visiting Hours

The house has the feeling of a hospital. The rooms are barely furnished. The air tastes sterile and everything smells like rubber gloves. I can see the lines the vacuum left behind on the carpet the same way I can see the path of the lawn mower on the front grass.

–You can wait in there– Rianna's mother says to me . . pointing to the room off the hallway where I can see two chairs set apart from each other. In the room on the other side there are two sofas and I get the message loud and clear that her mother doesn't want me too near her daughter even if it's only for sitting.

–Okay . . thanks– I say after I clear the cotton feeling in my throat.

I move into the waiting room.

Her mother calls upstairs for Rianna and then pokes her head back into the room where she has placed me . . gives me a fake smile and then walks off. I listen to the sound of her shoes as they fade away.

Her family is poor.

It isn't obvious in the way it's obvious that my mother is poor. Their house isn't run-down . . isn't any smaller than the other houses in town. Her family is a different kind of poor . . too proud to show it wherever it is possible to cover it up with vacuums and lawn mowers and wood furniture so well polished that I can see my pale nervous reflection in the shine.

I feel the way I used to feel at the doctor's office when I would sit on the paper-covered table in my underwear waiting for the doctor to come in.

I try to imagine what she'll be wearing when she comes into the room. I've never seen her wear anything besides the same four shirts and jeans . . sometimes a dark blue one . . sometimes a light blue sweatshirt instead . . sometimes one that zippers in the front and other times just one that pulls over.

There should be no reason to think she would come down in anything else but I can't stop picturing her in a torn white robe the way Lacie would have drawn her if she were making a portrait.

I wonder if I should have worn something else?

I caught the disapproving look on her mother's face when she answered the door . . working her way from my wild hair down to the scuffed boots and jeans where holes have worn their way through at the knees. I wonder who the last boy to visit Rianna on a Sunday was and what he might have worn and if her mother was comparing me to him and knowing that I don't stack up well.

My heart beats with the sound of her feet.

Down one step . . down the next.

I look for a place to put my hands . . resting them on the armrests of the chair . . folded in front of my stomach . . finally placing them under my knees when I see her shadow in the doorway.

Her hair is pulled back in a ponytail so I don't recognize her at first . . no baggy sweatshirt over her leotard so tight that I can see the shape of her ribs beneath. She is wearing jeans though . . frayed at the bottom where her bare feet stick out.

–Hi!– she says with a big smile . . a real smile not like her mother's smile and I can't help but smile back even though I hate the way I look when I smile.

–I just got home. I didn't shower yet– she says . . and her smile turns to a frown as she looks down at herself in disgust.

–That's okay– I tell her. *–I don't mind.–* I'm trying not to stare at the shape of her breasts.

Rianna shrugs her shoulders and throws her arms to her side . . *–Okay then–* she says and comes into the room . . sitting on the chair facing the one I'm in. She pulls her legs

up and sits with them folded under her the way kindergart-
ners sit when they are called to sit in circles for storytime.

The sound from the television comes through the
walls . . the sound of her father cheering when something
good happens in the game he is watching . . Rianna laughs
and apologizes for him. I tell her my dad's the same way and
then we both go silent searching for words to say to each
other.

–*How was practice?*–

It is the only thing that comes into my head as I look at
the straps of her leotard digging into her shoulders . . leaving pink lines on her skin . . red-and-white-printed stripes
that crisscross her body like an *X* marking a treasure map.

–*Okay I guess*– she says and then twists her arm around to
look at the underneath side . . –*I fell on the beam*– and points
to a purple bruise that threatens to swallow her entire arm.

I touch my face quickly before pulling my hand away.

My bruise faded away weeks and weeks ago but I can
still feel it sometimes if I touch my face . . I can still feel
where his fist crushed against my bone.

–*Does it hurt?*– I ask.

Rianna shakes her head . . says she's used to it.

–*How long have you been . . training?*– hoping that is
the right word . . it seems better than *practicing* or *gymnas-
ticing.*

104

−I don't know . . since I was three I think− and I try to imagine her as a child falling over mats and laughing as she tumbles into other laughing kids.

There are shelves on every wall . . all of them covered with trophies . . some are silver . . some gold . . some large and others only plaques that are hung beside the shelves alongside ribbons of every color.

−You must be really good− I say as my eyes travel around the room.

−Mmmm hmmm− she says but not in a way that feels like she is bragging . . more like she's uninterested . . still studying the bruise on her arm and not looking at the trophies that she must get sick of seeing.

−What about you?− she says. *−How long have you been writing in notebooks?−* and I can feel my face turn red because I've never written in one in front of her or told her about them at all and since I don't know how she knows I'm instantly terrified that somehow she's read them . . read the stories I've written about her . . even though it's impossible I can't help thinking it's true.

−I've watched you write in them . . at lunch . . in class . . you write in them all the time.− She laughs . . smiling at how shy I am about it. I stutter . . still too startled to know what to say. *−It's okay . . you don't have to tell me if you don't want to.−*

105

–Um . . no . . uh . . I don't know. A long time I guess. Since my mom and I moved away from Dad.–

–Oh– she says . . says she's sorry . . she didn't mean anything by bringing it up . . and I tell her it's fine. Then she asks me where my dad lives and I tell her that I'm back here living with him now. She looks confused by the whole thing but doesn't want to ask me any more about it because I guess she can see that I don't really want to talk about all that anyway.

–So what do you write in them . . the notebooks?–

–Just things– I say and hope to God that she doesn't ask me to let her read them. I would have to say no . . I would have to hide my secrets . . but I'm not sure I could say no to anything she asks me . . not with those eyes . . not with the way she touches the side of her face.

–Good things?– she asks.

–Sometimes– I say . . not wanting to tell her about the bad things.

–Good.– She looks down at the bruise on her arm again as I look at the straps digging into her shoulders. I want only to get up and go over to her . . stand behind her and pull the straps down onto her arms and make the indentations go away by tracing them with my fingers.

She looks up at me . . lifting her head so quickly that I'm afraid that maybe I've done something wrong because she looks startled.

I look down at my hands resting in my lap.

–*You wanna go for a walk or something?*– she asks. It takes a moment for the words to make sense . . the words don't fit her expression . . from the look on her face I thought she was angry about something but the tone of her voice is so soft . . so hopeful . . and I realize even more than I realized before that she is the strangest girl that I've ever met in that way . . stranger even than Lacie because at least with Lacie I always knew what she would say when she opened her mouth to speak.

–*Okay*– looking directly into her eyes for the first time.

–*Great. I just have to run upstairs and get a sweater.*– She jumps up from her chair and I get up more slowly to follow her . . but she stops at the doorway . . holds her hand up like a crossing guard . . –*You have to wait here*– she whispers . . her voice so serious . . so stern that I freeze. Even when she tries to hide it with a faint smile I stay still.

–*I'll be right back*– she says . . her voice more normal again. I watch as she leaps two steps at a time.

We only step onto the shoulder of the road when a car approaches . . otherwise we walk along the center line . . against the traffic . . side by side. I don't ask her where we're going. I don't care. As long as she is beside me anyplace seems okay.

–*Sorry about earlier . . in my house*– she says . . looking down at her old sneakers as she walks. –*I'm not really allowed to have anyone in my room . . especially boys.*– She looks up at me. –*I'm not really allowed to have boys over at all . . I told my mom that you were a friend coming over. I didn't tell her you were a boy.*–

My stomach begins to lift and drop . . I wish I'd known because maybe then I could have met her somewhere else.

–*Are you going to get in trouble?*– I ask.

Rianna shrugs her shoulders . . –*Maybe . . probably.*–

–*I'm sorry*– I whisper and stop walking.

–*No . . it's not your fault*– she says and stops with me . . steps toward me and puts her hands on my hands . . then lets go quickly.

She starts to walk again . . her shadow longer now than when we left . . the sun lower in the sky behind us and we walk away from where all the stores are in town and toward the park with its promise of spring flowers and tree blossoms and benches where we don't have to sit so far apart.

I follow her . . silent . . careful not to get too close as she twists the string of her sweatshirt's hood around and around her finger until the tip turns purple and she lets it fall loose again.

–*My parents are sooo protective!*– she bursts out . . clenching her hands into fists at her side like an angry child . . raising her voice so that the old couple walking out of the park turn their heads in our direction . . frown . . then walk off the other way.

My friend Avery would know exactly what to do . . he'd know if she wanted me to put my arm around her and he'd know what exactly I should say to her. He would know if I should keep my distance and let her calm down and smile again before touching the back of her neck lightly with my fingernails.

But I'm not Avery . . I can't tell at all what girls want. So

I stand behind her and put my hands in my pockets feeling helpless and stupid.

I stop walking when she stops.

She looks so small . . like someone made to fit on the tiny balance beam that she practices walking on so much.

–I hate them sometimes– she says . . her eyes sad and dark . . and that is when I stop thinking . . stop trying to figure out what is right and wrong . . what I should do or what Avery would do and I walk over to her and slip my hands under her sweatshirt and they slide easily over the nylon and lock together behind the small of her back.

I wait for her to look at me . . to push the loose strands of her hair away from her mouth before I kiss her.

I open my mouth and feel all of her pain flow inside of me as I hold mine down deep to protect her because I know there are times when even angels need someone to protect them too . . when they need a break from healing and need to be healed themselves.

We feel like two trees that have grown together . . our roots twisted around each other like snakes tied in knots under the ground. Each branch lying against the others . . each leaf softly petting other leaves as we try to swallow each other's seeds because seeds are like secrets that will keep us together forever.

And for an instant we are one person before separating.

The wind picks up as we pull away from each other.

–*I'm . . I didn't . .* – I stutter. Rianna smiles and lowers her eyes . . her hand wiping gently at the corner of her mouth where my saliva left traces.

I have this weird feeling inside me like wanting time to speed up so that the rest of our lives could happen right this second . . wanting a lifetime with her all at once.

–*Kiss me again*– she says . . but as I lean in she pushes away and wiggles out of my arms. –*You have to catch me first*– . . her voice trailing away in the wind as she starts to run so fast through the empty park.

I stand stunned for a second with my hands beside me . . confused at the way she changes mood faster than the sky before a thunderstorm. I'm not used to feeling so different so quickly . . my feelings take longer to move away from me . . I watch her . . amazed at what a beautiful thing it must be to have that ability.

–*Better hurry!*– she shouts as she starts to run up the hill.

And I know she really is an angel now as I start to run because my feet feel like clouds that move across the sun . . not even noticing my arms as they swing back and forth at my side or the burning feeling in my lungs . . remembering what it felt like to be a child as I ran over playgrounds . . remembering how easy everything felt then and remembering that I forgot that I could ever feel that way again. It must be how she feels all the time. Safe and free. I don't want to catch her if it means this feeling will ever go away.

But she keeps calling me . . keeps slowing down . . letting me get closer . . the taste of her lip gloss like candy in my mouth as I run . . and I run faster because I want the feel of my arms around her again.

Rianna is standing on top of the hill.

She isn't running anymore. She is watching me run.

She points at me and laughs.

I laugh with her . . out of breath as I try to make it up the last few steps.

—You know I'm letting you catch me . . right?— she says as she puts her arms together. I nod . . I never would have caught her.

Her hand reaches out to pull me into her and we both fall to the ground as our bodies meet.

As we breathe our rib cages move up and down like waves on the ocean.

Our hands are sweaty as they hold on to each other's.

She spreads her arms like featherless wings across the ground . . an open invitation . . a whispered one as I move over the grass and dirt to be beside her first . . to move my body on top of hers next as she closes her eyes . . her mouth slightly parted . . soft sounds escaping . . sounds begging to be spoken inside me as I cover her mouth with mine and we begin speaking without words.

I close my eyes and imagine that the birds are all gathering above us . . circling around and making a spiral astronomy.

Something about the way she tastes of bubble gum . . the way she smells of sour vanilla sweat . . the way her body feels safely pinned beneath me makes it impossible for either of us to stop smiling.

—*What?*— she says . . giggling . . —*What is it?*— because I can't stop smiling and have to stop kissing.

—*Nothing . . just happy*— I say . . and she says —*Me too*— and pulls me in closer to her again.

Sometimes I don't know what's wrong with me.

Sometimes I think that maybe I deserve everything bad that happens to me.

That's how I feel when Lacie answers the phone . . her voice like elementary school kids singing Christmas songs . . so happy and so open and fragile.

–*I miss you*– she says . . and I feel numb and stupid on the other end of the line.

I called to tell her about Rianna . . how I just spent the most perfect afternoon with her.

I wanted to tell Lacie how Rianna reminds me of the girl in her drawings. I wanted to tell her that I've found an angel and that I think I'm going to be okay. But then when I hear her voice I no longer want to speak.

I don't know what made me think it would make her happy to hear all these things. I guess I didn't think about it. I only thought about how happy it would make me feel to tell someone who I could share secrets with.

–Benji . . are you still there?– she asks.

I make a quiet noise.

–I miss you– she says again . . and I tell her I miss her too.

It's not a lie . . I keep telling myself it's not a lie because I do miss her. But if it's so goddamned true then why can't I stop thinking of Rianna's smile every time I try to picture Lacie lying on her bed with the phone pressed so closely to her ear that I know my silence hurts her.

–How is it . . with your dad?–

–Good . . I guess.– And I hate myself for wanting only to find a reason to get off the phone . . to sort out everything in my head and call her back when my stomach isn't so confused inside.

–Guess what– she says . . I don't even try to guess . . I feel too sick to speak . . wait silently long enough for her to tell me. *–My mom says I can come visit you once school's out!–* and the happiness in her voice makes me pinch the skin on my wrist so tight that I can feel my fingernails cutting into it.

–Really? That's great.– But I can't even make myself believe the excitement is real let alone Lacie who is the only person who has ever been able to understand me.

We are both silent for what feels like a few minutes.

The sound of her breathing is like the feeling of a fist striking me over and over again . . hitting harder each time until I feel like I might faint when she asks me *–What's wrong?–*

–Nothing– . . but the word is as empty as it sounds. *– Look Lacie . . I have to go . . my dad is calling me. I just wanted to say hi–* but that is a lie. I have to go because if I don't I feel like maybe my lungs will collapse.

–Okay– she says . . and I wonder if she can tell . . if she knows everything already without me having to tell her because she has always had that gift.

–I'll call you later this week . . okay? I promise.– And I can hear her nodding her head . . I can hear by the muffled way she breathes that she has put her fingers up to her mouth . . that her eyes are staring off into the distance . . cloudy . . spotting of rain and I have to hang up the phone now or I will never be able to live with myself.

–I love you– she says. I tell her that I love her too knowing that I will spend the rest of my life trying to figure out if I'm telling the truth.

I wait for the other end to go quiet before I hang up.

I wait to catch my breath.

I wait to wipe my eyes until after I have thrown the phone across the room . . screaming like I'm throwing something very heavy . . grunting as I put my entire body into it the way I never did when throwing a baseball the way my dad told me to.

–STUPID . . FUCKING . . THING!–

The plastic cracks against the wall. My dog whines and lowers his ears as he sneaks past me and out of my room.

I fall onto my bed.

I used to always wish my stuffed animals could come to life when I was little. It seemed so easy on television for things like that to happen. It seemed if I only pleaded hard enough . . kept my hands folded and my eyes shut and spoke up to the ceiling that eventually it would come true. I tried for days on end to be good . . to not get in trouble . . to do extra things for my mother like clean the kitchen without being told . . hoping she would recognize the shiny counter as she took down a new glass and poured herself a new drink.

She never noticed.

My stuffed animals never came to life.

I used to think that I must have done something wrong for my wishes not to come true . . I must be bad . . or at least worse than the boys on tv whose toys came alive or who got to travel accidentally through time while I was stuck in my miserable life forever.

Maybe I was never meant to be special.

But then . . when I met Lacie . . everything felt different.

She felt more like one of those special things on tv than like a person . . like a doll that had come to life . . like an angel that had come down to find me . . protect me.

I never want to hurt her.

I would rather die instead. I could follow her like a ghost living beneath the wallpaper in her bedroom.

Dying would be less painful.

Dying would be easy because it is something I can control.

Feelings aren't so easy. I can't control them . . I can't make myself feel in love with her the way I want to . . because that is only how my brain is telling me to feel . . but my heart is telling me to feel a different way. But none of that means I don't love her . . none of it means I've forgotten about her . . or that I don't need her.

I do love her.

I just love someone else too.

I love her . . but not the same.

But I will never be able to explain anything of this without hurting her . . without making her think she did something wrong . . that she isn't good enough. And if I am someone who can make Lacie feel that way . . then maybe I am trash.

–*What's going on in here?*–

I don't take my face away from the pillow but I don't have to . . I know it's my dad standing at the door . . his

118

arms folded . . his face red the way cops get on the television when no one is giving them straight answers.

I wish he would go away.

I wish I could disappear.

–*Goddammit . .*– and I know he has seen the phone cracked on the floor. He's so predictable. Maybe that's why I've never been able to understand him because complicated people are easier to know.

–*Hey! What the hell is going on?*–

I look at him for the first time . . turning my head to the side so that he can see me crying . . can see snot on my face like a *wimpy-ass little kid.*

–*MY LIFE SUCKS! THAT'S WHAT! YOU HAPPY NOW?*–

It is the first time I have ever really yelled at him . . yelled in a way that doesn't hold anything back . . that scratches the back of my throat as the words come out. He is too shocked to even change his expression.

My mother wouldn't have been shocked . . not at all. She and I would yell that way at least twice a week. That's why I cover my face with my arms . . brace myself for something breakable.

I'm ready for him to hurt me.

I'm ready for any punishment he can give out.

–*Jesus*– my dad says . . dropping his arms to his side . . changing his expression as his eyes go soft around the edges . . covering his mouth with one hand and saying –*Jesus*– again into his palm because maybe he's realizing for the first time in his life that mine is completely fucked up.

–*Just leave me alone!*– I bury my face in my pillow again . . crossing my fingers beneath me . . hoping he will leave but knowing he won't.

He whispers something to Janet as I hear her asking –*What's wrong? What is it?*– over and over again and my dad telling her it's okay before the door clicks secure behind him.

His steps make the floor creak as he walks toward me.

–*Hey . . hey sport*– he says as he sits down on the corner of my bed and I can't help but laugh into my pillow . . fucking *sport* . . I'm the one who should be saying –*Jesus*– over and over to myself.

I promise myself not to look at him.

Not to speak to him.

Ignore him until he goes away.

But then when his hand touches my back it feels like tiny daggers stabbing me up and down my spine . . like a thousand insects with pincers biting me at once and I jump up and back away from him with my knees pulled up to my chest.

–*Don't touch me!*– I bark . . –*Never touch me!*–

My father's hand stays suspended in the air above where my back was moments ago.

–It's all right . . hey . . Benji . . it's okay– he says . . motioning with his hands for me to calm down . . speaking slowly like I'm some psycho who should be tied up so I don't move from my bed.

–I'm fine– I say . . fine now . . my hair hiding my face . . my eyes glowing like stars exploding . . like tiger eyes at night.

–You want to tell me what's going on?– my dad asks and I shake my head . . whisper *–nothing–* with my tongue pressing against my teeth.

My dad looks down at the dead phone and then looks back to me.

–Who was that? Sean?–

–No.– And I hate how he thinks everything in my life has to do with the one or two things he's bothered to learn about me. Sean is the only name he knows . . therefore Sean is to blame for everything. I wish he wouldn't guess at knowing.

–Then who?– he says. *–Hey . . I'm here . . I'm listening.–*

But I still don't feel like talking.

I don't feel like ever talking to him about anything . . can't he understand that?

I'd rather just write everything down . . keep it safe between the pages of my notebook . . keep it to myself on paper. He can read it when I'm dead . . he can learn then when I don't have to watch his face.

–Who . . was . . it?– he repeats . . speaking the way he

121

always did when I was a kid . . when he found out something wrong I did but would make me tell him anyway . . even when he *knew* he had to make me say it.

–*A girl*– . . the words wet with the sound of snot in my throat.

–*Ohhh*– he says like he understands everything now. I give him a look so that he knows not to do that . . not to boil my life down to some bullshit teenage drama about a crush . . not to give me that smirk like he fucking knows all about my life now that I've told him one little fact.

And for the first time in my life I get the feeling that he gets the message. His expression changes . . he says –*sorry*– . . means it . . says –*Hey . . I'm sorry*– . . asks if I want to talk about it.

–*Why?*–

Does he want me to be his best friend now . . one apology and he wants me to forget that he never really loved me that much?

–*Because maybe I can help*– he tells me and I roll my eyes. –*Try me . . I wasn't born this age you know.*–

I try to picture my dad being my age but I've only ever seen one picture of him when he was a kid and he was much younger than I am and he didn't look anything like he does now . . didn't look anything like me either and so I can't imagine it the right way.

I shake my head. I don't want to tell him about Lacie.

I don't want him to ask me about her . . about what she's like . . about the things I like about her . . the things she likes about me. I don't want to hear him patronize me . . to tell me I'm overreacting . . that *when you get older you'll see what I mean* type of shit.

–It can be tough– he says.

I think about when he and my mom split . . how it didn't seem tough for him . . not the way it was tough for her and me.

–Yeah . . I guess.–

He nods his head up and down . . *–Your guess is right–* . . and then he gives that far-off smile that he gives whenever he thinks he's said something clever.

–I just want to be alone now– I say . . still backed into the corner on my bed . . still holding my knees close to me because I'm afraid to let them go.

–Okay– my dad says . . tells me he understands.

I let him think that . . let him think his little talk has helped because it's easier than explaining the truth to him.

As he is about to leave my room he stops.

–Benji?– he says to get me to look at him . . keeps his eyes on my eyes . . studies me . . I give away nothing. *–Whenever you want to talk . . well . . you know . . okay?–*

–Sure Dad– . . and I smile at him the way I smile at teachers . . smile to please him but the smile doesn't show anything that I have inside of me.

Wanting to Throw It All Away

The music is like a theater deep inside a cave that puts on a performance of what hell looks like . . peeling the color from the rocks.

The singer's voice is a painful scream over the music.

It is the growling voice of a demon dying through the headphones.

Loud.

Angry.

But there is a sadness there too and that sadness is me . . that is where I find comfort in the music. It surrounds the sadness and keeps it protected from anger and hate.

It is the same with scary movies. I watch them because they keep the evil behind the glass of the television where it can't come out to get me. I can be safe keeping the demons near me but separate. I can disappear in the blue electricity of the television . . fade to white outlines . . burn off like fog . . let the nightmares play out there instead of inside.

The bus moves like the road is being hit by small earthquakes . . my teeth chattering with the last frost on the window . . hitting over the bumps and breaks in the asphalt.

The trees fade away too as soon as we pass them. The tires always pulling the distance closer to me . . pushing everything else farther behind.

The soundtrack running in my ears . . electrical current traveling faster than the bus and bringing information in the form of music that sounds like hell . . I try to imagine the end of the world as we drive. I can't hear anything except the terrified sound of the song.

I can see the other kids move their lips . . the girl in front of me talking to the girl next to her. I can see their words but I can't hear them . . the sound like a wolf howling covers me and I like that I'm the only one who can hear them screaming.

I've been ignoring Rianna all day.

I've been trying to think of things I hate about her.

I hate her friends . . girls like Cam who wear designer clothes and wait for people to compliment her so that she can brag about how much they cost or how they are the newest thing out there.

I hate how Rianna doesn't hate them the way I do . . how she lets them make her think they are better than her and how she thinks being like them is being normal.

I hate how she acts sometimes like she isn't thinking about anything at all when I can tell from her eyes that she is.

I want to hate her so that next time I talk to Lacie I can tell her that I love her and only her.

But the more reasons I come up for hating Rianna the more I realize that those are also the reasons why I like her.

Butterflies begin to buzz in my stomach as I walk to my class because there is no way to avoid her anymore. She will be waiting for me . . waiting for me to talk to her . . wondering if we are going to act differently with each other now . . if I'm going to act like her boyfriend or not.

I won't do that.

I won't start acting like those couples in the hallway who hang all over each other . . who need everyone to see them together so that they don't feel alone.

I won't force stupid conversations before class starts.

I don't want to think about whether or not I'm supposed to sit next to her today instead of sitting a few desks away like I always do.

Those are things that I really do hate . . and I try to tell myself that she is to blame for all those things . . for the butterflies in my stomach . . for feeling awkward . . for feeling guilty.

I see her outside the classroom as I get near . . with a friend of hers I don't know . . looking down the hall and I can tell she is looking for me so I make sure to walk slowly behind a group of guys who are all taller than I am.

Every thought of her I've had today has been so full of hate that when I see her I don't feel the way I normally do . . I don't see the angel that lives behind her smile or the softness in her eyes. I see her flaws . . the way her freckles are a bit too big . . the way her hair hasn't been washed again and hangs there like dying weeds.

–*Hi!*– she says once I can no longer hide . . her voice happy like a song . . it annoys me because I want it to.

Her friend annoys me . . laughing . . covering her mouth . . waiting to see us kiss or hold hands or anything that will announce that we are boyfriend and girlfriend after yesterday.

–*Hey*– making my voice like the growling demons that play inside my headphones. I don't stop . . I only slow down for a second to look at her with angry eyes before pushing past and into the classroom where I sit as far away from her as I possibly can.

I let the demons inside me take over . . let them grow stronger for a short while . . just long enough so that I can take pleasure in seeing the shocked look on Rianna's face from the doorway . . just long enough to be able to smile to myself when I see that maybe she is about to cry when she comes in and sees me sitting on the opposite side of the room.

The class can't go by fast enough for me.

It takes forever.

Our teacher is talking and talking about things that I'm not listening to because I'm trying so hard only to look forward . . to not let my head glance over at her . . to not let myself be honest . . trying to convince myself that I'm over her . . that my interest in her was only a mistake.

Rianna stares at me from across the room the way I used to stare at her. I can feel her staring . . covering me like smoke . . burning my skin slowly until I turn red but I know I can't look at her because the demons have worn off and I will only be able tell her I'm sorry if I look her in the eyes.

The entire world conspires against me as I try to leave the room . . the teacher holds us ten seconds after the bell rings to finish assigning homework . . the girl in front of me drops her pen . . her book . . and then her notes on four loose leaves of paper.

Rianna packs her things up slowly . . calmly . . and I look over at her and then at the girl in front of me and help her by picking up the pen at least before pushing by her.

Rianna leaves her row and I head for the door and it is like a track race where the people on the outside lanes look so much closer to the finish than the ones on the inside until it comes toward the end.

Two people stand talking to each other at the front of my row . . two Neanderthals that I do not particularly wish to fight through.

By the time I get into the hallway . . into the deafening

roar of voices and lockers being opened and closed . . it's too late. Rianna is right behind me . . tapping me on the shoulder so that to ignore her would be even more obnoxious than I could ever be.

–*Hi*– I say. She narrows her eyes expecting more words to come from me . . getting angry when they don't follow.

–*You're not going to walk with me?*– she asks. Her voice seems so small . . the way Polly's does when I break a promise to her.

–*Um . . okay . . I'll walk*– I say . . but today she doesn't smile like she normally would and I don't slow down or move aside to let her walk beside me . . feeling better with her behind me where I can't see her.

Passing through the door is like walking into the bright light of death . . the sun is so bright outside that I have to look down until my eyes adjust . . the feel of spring all around me even in the cement. Rianna uses that time to step around me . . in front of me where she stops and puts her hands on my chest to make me stop too.

I look to the side of her . . notice the plants growing wild up the brick walls . . the grass like an ocean of green out on the fields . . the trees full . . the air warm and I notice for the first time that spring is actually almost gone . . that summer will be here soon with its own smells and feelings.

–*Maybe I should just go*– I say . . staring out into the landscape and its promise of nothingness.

–*What did I do?*– Rianna asks . . this time crying . . without noise though . . only with tears.

–*What?*– . . trying to sound like I don't know what she means . . like she's misread me . . trying to make her believe that I haven't been acting horrible to her all day . . trying to make myself believe it too because I hate that I'm making her eyes get wet around the edges.

–*Why do you hate me now?*– She takes her hands away from me and puts them near her eyes to wipe the tears out of the corners.

–*I don't hate you*– I say . . I hate myself . . I hate myself more and more every second we stand here because I won't let myself put my hands on her face like I want to . . won't let my fingers trace the freckles under her eyes until she smiles and then we can forget about every stupid thing I've done today.

–*Then why are you being like this!*– It is the first time I've heard her voice so fierce and it startles me.

–*I . . I don't know . . I'm sorry*–because I don't know . . at this minute I don't . . I can't remember anything but the look in her eyes . . on her face when for a second she thought I hated her when I could never hate her from now until I die. Everything inside me is so confused . . running together the way the colors mix in dirty water when you clean paintbrushes . . the reds no longer red . . the blue turning brown as everything else turns brown when it touches the water. None of my feelings are separate any-more . . my feelings for Rianna or Lacie . . my feelings about this place and the place I moved from . . my feelings about the demons and the angels.

–Benji . . I like you . . if . . – and she pauses to get up the courage to tell me how she feels. I can't even look her in the eyes as she speaks . . *–If you don't like me . . tell me right now–* she says and she isn't crying anymore . . she is standing up straight . . the strength in her muscles showing through everywhere to let me know she is strong.

Suddenly everything feels empty . . the trees seem like toys placed in a shoe box for show . . the school nothing but a backdrop on a stage. Even the birds seem like an after-thought . . put there to decorate the blank sky and give people something to look at.

Rianna is the only thing that feels real.

She is the only thing that is alive.

She is more alive than everything else added up and mul-tiplied together and I realize for the first time that it is the life inside her that I'm attracted to . . the thing that is inside her and makes her eyes glow from behind the glassy cover.

And I realize that hurting her is not going to keep Lacie from being hurt . . that hurt will happen either way . . that hurt was determined the minute I first saw Rianna.

–I'm sorry– I say again . . whisper . . *–I . . I . . –* but noth-ing that comes out of my mouth seems right so I touch her

face instead . . and she turns her cheek into my hand before putting her hand over mine as she begins to walk again . . leading me to the gym . . both of us careful not to speak . . both of us aware that nothing has been settled yet.

–Do you like me?– she asks again when we are outside the door.

–It's just that . . I'm . . I'm kind of a fuck-up . . you know?– I answer . . because it's true . . I fuck everything up . . and inside me everything is fucked up like rusty metal rotting in a junkyard.

And it's my turn to let my eyes cloud over and her turn to look away toward the trees that are planted neatly in a row between the school building and the parking lot where kids are still screwing around and blasting competing music into the sound of engines that aren't going anywhere.

Then Rianna looks at me . . smiling the way I'm used to seeing her smile . . playful . . a little streak of something mischievous . . *–Yeah I know–* she says . . then lowers her eyes . . looks up at me . . twists her hair around her finger . . *–But do you like me?–*

I nod.

Over and over.

–Call me tonight? After practice?– she says and I nod again.

–Promise?–

–Promise.–

Spies in Scenery

Sean is waiting for me around the other side of the school. Keith is with him. Another kid too. I know his face . . a friend of Keith's . . Jared or Jordan I think. I met him once in a group of a lot of people so I'm not sure . . just that he's older . . a junior.

The three of them are careful to stand exactly off the property of the school so they can smoke cigarettes without any teachers or principal coming over to tell them what they can and can't do . . here they can point to the ground at an imaginary line where the rules of Covington Senior High come to an end.

–*Hey!*– holding up my hand as I cross over the line to where they are standing. Sean is holding out a cigarette for me to take . . lighter lit . . and I don't really want one so I shake my head.

–What . . you quit already?– Keith says. His friend laughs.

Sean shrugs and puts the cigarette back loose in his pocket . . lets the flame burn out and puts the lighter in his pocket too.

–You remember Jordan?– Keith says and I nod. Jordan doesn't. He wears a look on his face that says he fully expects me to remember him . . that who the fuck am I to forget him because he's Jordan and I'm just the new kid . . just fucking Dogboy.

–Come on . . let's go– Sean says and turns away . . starts walking into the wind with a sudden burst of momentum.

He gets about ten steps ahead of us before we gather ourselves enough to follow.

–Are we going to the shed?– I ask.

–Fuck that!– Jordan says.

–Nah . . we're going over to where they're building that shopping center . . over on Church Street. We can get into the building from the back– Keith tells me.

We walk along the road for a while . . keeping our feet just on the inside of the white line that marks the road from the overgrown weeds beside it. The cars have to swerve into the oncoming lane to make room for us. Most of the people driving give us dirty looks as they pass . . as they turn the steering wheel and slow down so that they can get around us. Sean doesn't seem to notice or care because he never turns to look at them and never takes even a half step over to the shoulder.

I notice though.

–*This way*.– Jordan turns off the road and into a newly planted field with hundreds of rows of short green sprouts that will grow through the summer into stalks of corn that will hide the distance from the sight of the road.

Mice dart across our path as we walk . . running from one row of plants to the next and the next and as many as it takes for them to feel safe from us as we walk like intruders through the field.

I feel like staying here . . sitting down in the dirt and part of me thinks I might be happy here . . waiting with the birds for something to happen . . waiting for the dead of night to cover over this little town and knowing that here I would be safe from ever having to make any decisions.

–*We cut through those woods there and we'll be right up behind the shopping center*– Jordan says to us . . taking the lead from Sean . . plowing ahead like the machines that plow under the crops in harvest season.

I don't say anything. I'm just along for the ride.

The door is made of a single sheet of plywood. It isn't nailed up properly and it's easy for us to push it aside enough to slide in.

The sounds of the busy road out front of the shopping center disappear as the board falls back into place . . sealing us off from the world the way a tomb would.

The sunlight turns gray and damp inside the building . . no place for it to get in except for a few windows high above where they've just begun to build a second floor.

Nothing has really happened yet inside the building. There are no stores laid out . . only a few walls to suggest where they might be but it is easy for us to move from one to the next and I think about how strange it will be to be inside here once it's open and to know that once there was nothing between the pizza place and the pharmacy.

Sean loses it the second we are safely inside.

He runs through the open space like a bird with amputated wings . . calling out at the top of his lungs . . screaming to take flight with his arms outstretched. His voice echoes off the walls the way thunder would sound trapped inside a jar . . fills every inch of space.

I'm about to join him . . thinking it will feel good to be so free for even a minute.

I'm ready to run with my hands at my sides when Jordan shouts from behind me . . –*KNOCK IT THE FUCK OFF!*– . . his voice echoing off the empty walls like rocks thrown through storefront windows.

Sean stops dead in his tracks.

–*You want to get us caught?*– Jordan says and Sean shakes his head and apologizes. I don't think he should have apologized.

–*Quit fucking around*– Jordan says and heads off toward the side farthest away from the road and the construction vehicles that sit in the parking lot. –*Let's go get high*– he says.

I wait for Sean to get over to where we are standing.

Keith and Jordan walk ahead of us . . part of me wishes they would walk away for good. Sean and I could run through the empty building yelling our names or childish rhymes or whatever else came into our heads.

–*What was going on with you and Rianna?*– Sean asks me . . quietly so that Keith and Jordan can't hear.

–What do you mean?– I say . . not knowing if he wants me to be honest or if he's just being polite.

–I saw you guys . . she looked upset.–

–Yeah . . it's okay now . . I think.– I don't want to get into everything . . not here . . not like this. Maybe some other time if he really cares.

–She's pretty cool– he says . . and I look at him but he is looking down at his feet so that I know he's being serious . . says he used to be friends with her when they were in elementary school . . before there were so many rules and cliques . . before it was unacceptable for them to talk to each other.

–What the hell are you two doing? Come on!– Keith says . . peeking around a half-built wall. Jordan is already lighting a bowl . . breathing deeply . . breathing more . . holding it in before letting a cloud of white smoke rise to the ceiling where electrical wires dangle.

–Who's next?– he says as he starts coughing. There is no ceremony to it . . none of the ritual that I've grown so accustomed to in the shed when it's just me and Keith and Sean.

I gesture to Keith for him to go ahead and he takes the pipe and lighter the way little kids take presents.

The weed seems to burn more quickly . . burning with the greed with which Keith swallows the taste of it.

He passes it with smoke still in his lungs.

146

I let Sean go ahead even though I know there might not be any left by the time it gets to me.

–It's kicked!– Sean says . . the lighter only touching on ash.

–You don't have to fucking whine about it.– Jordan takes the bowl from Sean's hand . . reaches into his pocket and fills it again. *–Here.–* He passes it to Sean again.

Breathe in.

Breathe out.

My turn now.

I take the lighter in my right hand.

The bowl in my left.

Quick spark of the flame and I think for a second that I can see demon bones behind Jordan's skin . . but the image fades as the fire enters my mouth.

I'm careful not to take too much . . aware that Jordan is looking at me . . wondering why the hell he is smoking up some boy he doesn't even know. *–Thanks–* I say as I pass it back to him . . following the rules of etiquette and all that.

We stay in formation as long as we can.

Keep the bowl moving from one to another as efficiently as possible but it all breaks down after four or five passes . . after the electrical wires begin to resemble snakes waiting above our heads to strike us . . after our faces turn to plastic masks of our own regular faces.

–I'm FUCKED up!– Keith says as his eyes travel back and forth . . studying the grid pattern of the cinder blocks.

–That's what the coke is there for– Jordan says . . a smile on his thin lips.

–Soda?– Sean says . . and Jordan laughs the way older kids always laughed at me when I was younger and wouldn't understand something they were talking about.

–Not soda dipshit . . *coke . . cocaine . . I put a little fucking turbo on that weed.–*

Sean's eyes are dull and scared the way I think my eyes must look if I could step outside of myself and see them. Jordan tells us both to *–relax . . it was only a sprinkle.–*

I can feel my heart racing inside me . . racing like it has been reborn with rabbit feet . . pounding against my ribs like my rabbit legs pound against the dirt in my dog dream.

It feels like a million tiny ants are crawling just below the surface of my skin and I wonder if it is real or if I'm only imagining it because I know there is something different about what I just did . . I wonder if I would have even noticed if Jordan hadn't said anything.

But everything I'm thinking about slowly begins to fade . . my mind dissolves as I stare up at the web of steel beams above my head . . the geometry of bricks and boards and how they come together to fit perfectly into walls.

The sound of the traffic becomes a ringing in my ears so

that after a while I don't even know if it's the traffic I hear
or just the ringing.

The sound of Sean's voice is like a cartoon in another
language . . interesting and strange but nothing that I can
understand.

Monday 5:11 pm

The air outside is strange. Everything is so clear that it feels more like a photograph than real life.

When I stare down at the pavement below me I have a vague feeling that I just fell . . but then I reach out to my sides and feel the wall . . reach forward and feel the empty space where the loading dock is up here on the loft.

I found the stairs leading up here by myself.

I looked behind me before I climbed them . . hoping maybe Sean was still with me. I'm not sure how we got split up . . not sure what happened after we got high. We all just seemed to drift off on our own.

I was chased up here by the howling of dogs inside the walls . . running in packs above my head . . balanced on the steel beams.

The stairs were here when they chased me . . waiting . . begging for me to climb them though they have no handrail and are only temporary and most likely dangerous to climb in my condition. I didn't see the stairs before . . not when I came in . . not when we wandered around.

The dogs quiet down when I'm alone . . when I'm safe up here and out of sight of everyone.

There's nothing in the loft except a few crates that are closed up. There is no wall on one side . . an open window onto the parking lot where the yellow construction vehicles are laid out like a little boy's toy trucks. An open invitation to jump . . to change my life today . . to silence the dogs forever when I land.

I stand on the edge . . leaning over . . wondering how far I can lean before I fall forward . . until I land two stories below with my face pressed against the pavement . . blood like pretty raindrops splattered across the blackness.

I can feel the sun on my face . . close my eyes and the backs of my eyelids glow red. It's hot enough to take off my jacket . . hot enough to let the sun warm the tiny hairs on my arms.

I keep my eyes closed as I undo the zipper and let my arms slip out . . let the jacket fall to my feet and keep count of the seconds it will take for the breeze to carry it off where it will dance in the air like floating trash on the highway. It's warm enough to lift my shirt up and let the air touch against my stomach.

Far-off shouts travel across the parking lot.

Distant words that have no meaning by the time they reach my ears.

With my eyes closed it's easy to imagine the noise comes from workers who aren't there . . an army of workers filing into the parking lot . . ready to start adding layer upon layer of brick and cement to this place . . ready to finish the job so that they can move on and build the next one and the next and all of them are the exact same thing with the exact same stores selling the exact same stuff so that it is easy to imagine all the workers with the same face . . the same half-shaved beard . . same hard hands that make fists easily.

I open my eyes and they are there like ghosts in the scenery . . sitting at the steering wheels . . at the controls of cranes and cement trucks and they have all stopped to see the boy . . the one in front is pointing at . . to see me . . to watch me show them my belly.

–*What are you doing up there boy?*– I imagine one of them yelling . . pointing at me . . a few of the others whistle at me as if I were a woman passing a construction site in an old movie and the rest laugh as if on command.

I don't say anything . . I don't want to talk to these ghosts.

I hide my face.

It is my time to fade.

It is my time to go far away . . retreat far inside myself.

The ghosts are whistling again . . shouting things

152

at me . . obscene things . . things they want me to do. Behind me the dogs begin to growl . . a low angry sound warning me to do whatever I'm told.

I listen but I go away . . I'm not here . . me . . Dogboy . . I'm far away and only Benji is here and I don't care what they do to him. I want them to do whatever they want to him . . drag him behind the trucks by ropes if they want . . just as long as they make him go away . . as long as they go away too when they are done and leave me alone forever.

My hands move down my sides . . my shirt slipping down from where I was holding it up. But there is no feeling in my hands . . they are numb as they undo the button of my jeans . . as they pull apart the ends so that the zipper peels to the sound of gnashing teeth.

I watch the ghosts holding their breath . . excitement on their ghost faces that all look like Roy's face as he leaned against my bedroom wall.

The waistband fits tight around my knees with my legs standing far apart . . my elbows at my sides like a scarecrow as I lift my shirt up again. The sound of the wind blowing through the leaves becomes the sound of applause and cat-calls and I can feel the blood rushing up my thighs as I grow bigger and the ghosts begin to laugh as I try to tell them with my eyes that it is only the warm air on my skin that is making it happen.

I turn around to face the wall the way their imaginary shouts tell me to and they respond with more imaginary applause . . more imaginary obscenities . . more promises of things they will want to do to me when I come down because they say I will have to come down eventually and that when I do they will be there waiting for me.

My shirt falls again as I lower my hands.

I lift it up again with my left hand.

I keep my right where it will make them happy . . touching softly like the feeling of the wind blowing over my body.

I don't want to but I do . . I smile for them . . make my eyes go all shy for them . . let my hair fall pretty around my face and perform for them.

I am like an angel on a stage above their heads . . performing in front of a window in the sky for demons that have gathered. But I'm not the kind of angel that Lacie or Rianna are . . I'm a dirty angel . . an angel the demons have caught . . a pet angel that they enjoy making into a wimpy-ass little kid who does what they tell him.

A group of birds on the ground gets suddenly frightened and takes off into the air . . cawing and screeching . . shattering the images of the ghosts below me. One by one I watch their faces crack like broken mirrors and dissolve into dust and again everything is clear like a photograph and I can see Keith staring up at me from the edge of the woods.

My heart almost explodes as I try to pull my pants up . . leaving my underwear bunched up and just being able to get the zipper up as my shirt falls down but not fast enough because when I look down Keith's face hasn't changed . . confused . . frightened . . disgusted . . but also something that shows he is unable to know just why he feels those things.

–*Just taking a piss*– I shout down to him . . my voice nervous and squeaky and Keith doesn't say a thing . . just turns away and walks back around the corner where he disappears from my sight the same way the ghosts did.

I rush back down the stairs behind me . . hoping to catch Keith alone . . hoping to be relaxed and able to joke with him about it . . tell him I was just taking a piss or if he doesn't believe that I can tell him it's the same thing as when we look at the porno magazines in the shed.

But he's not alone when I reach the first floor . . Jordan is standing with him. Keith is saying something to him but stops when he sees me.

–*What?*– I ask as they are both looking at me and then they both laugh.

–*Nothing*– Jordan says . . but says it like there is a lot behind that word . . that there's plenty but they are going to keep to themselves what they think about me and somehow that feels worse than if they just called me a pussy or something and let it go.

–It's pretty cool up there– I say . . because I have to try to get things normal again . . thinking if I act like nothing happened then Jordan won't be so convinced that Keith wasn't exaggerating.

–I bet it is– Keith says. I ask him what that's supposed to mean. He shakes his head and giggles the way Polly does when she has a secret that she can't wait to tell the whole world and I know if I make one wrong step or say one wrong thing the rest of today that Keith is going to do exactly that . . tell the rest of the world what he saw me doing so that the kids at school will think I'm even more a freak than they already do.

–Come on . . let's get out of here– Jordan says and starts walking out of the unfinished shopping center. *–This place sucks–* he says . . and for once I sort of agree with him.

–Where's Sean?– I ask. Keith says he's already waiting outside and there is something about the way he says it that makes me calm down inside . . something that says to me that he was only fucking with me . . that he has already forgotten and it's not a big deal what he saw me doing. At least I can hope that.

I walk outside and begin to breathe easier.

I walk outside and notice that I'm still completely stoned.

Janet is waiting by the kitchen window as I walk up to the house. The look on her face scares me . . like somebody has died and she is waiting for me to come home so she can tell me . . like she has been worried for me because I've been gone so long already without knowing.

I think about Lacie's dad.

How she told me he looked when she found him dead.

I think about how if something so terrible can happen so easily to her then much worse things are certain to happen to me.

I rush up to the house. *–Dad? Is my dad here?–* I ask. Janet shakes her head.

I try to look around her but she is standing in the doorway and my stomach feels all sick inside . . wondering what's behind her . . wondering if I should cry or if I should

157

run . . the way an animal must feel being brought into a cage for the first time.

–*Benji we need to talk*– she says . . and if there is something she needs to say to me then I don't want to play her stupid games. I'm not a little boy . . I don't need to be cradled . . I just need to know what's going on.

–*Where's my dad?*– I'm shouting at her and she says he's at work and seems surprised by my expression. So am I . . knowing now that it has nothing to do with him . . and I feel a little bit scared that I cared so much.

–*Benji?*– . . and this time it is Janet's eyes that are shaky . . her voice that is nervous as she looks at me and I can't help but think of my mom.

–*Is it her? Is it my mom?*– I ask. Janet shakes her head and lets me get around her.

I feel so stupid when I see my journals laid out on the kitchen table . . naked and open . . all three of them open to different pages.

Then I know why she is so surprised.

Then I know the reason she looked at me the way she did.

I can tell by looking at the words that they've been read . . the feel of someone else's eyes on them like the impressions left by pressing too hard on the pen.

I don't know if she has read every word and I don't care. She's read enough . . even one word is too much and I feel like my legs are on fire . . my chest . . every part of me is filled with a burning.

–*Is this . .*– Janet says through her fingers . . her hand in front of her face to block the words and the other hand motioning to the pages that I've filled with things that were always meant to stay private forever or until I died. –. . *Is it all true?*–

I grab them . . all three of them at once . . bunching them up so that pages get wrinkled as they shuffle together like large playing cards.

–*Is it true?*– she asks me again . . her hand away from her face . . her expression trying its hardest to appear normal . . calm . . and I scream at it . . at her face . . at the way it's looking at me like something is *FUCKING WRONG WITH ME!*

–*WHO SAID YOU COULD READ THESE?*– and I hold them so close to me . . so tight . . trying to see if I can pull everything she read away from her just by squeezing the pages to my body.

–*I didn't mean anything by it . . I just . . we were concerned and . .*– she says . . says she's sorry but I don't care. I don't care if she's sorry or not . . I don't care if she says now I can talk to her about it if I want . . now that she knows . . now that the hard part is over.

But I didn't tell her!

Doesn't she understand that it makes a difference?

To me it makes a difference.

I didn't let her know me . . she stole it.

–*Well I made it all up . . okay? It's just a story . . all right? Happy?*– and I pick my backpack up off the floor . . open it . . shove my notebooks inside.

Janet follows me as I walk to my room . . she doesn't come inside but I'm only grabbing one or two things so it doesn't matter . . I walk past her in the hallway again before she even has a chance to come in.

I'm not staying here.

Not anymore. Not tonight anyway.

I have to get away . . I have to get away from this house . . from her . . from the feeling of knowing my secrets are not secrets anymore. I will die if I stay here . . the demons will snatch me up without my secrets protected.

At least one secret is still safe . . those pages have been torn out . . at least that . . still nobody knows that.

–*Where are you going?*– Janet asks but I don't answer.

–*Look at me . . where are you going?*– but I walk faster to the door.

–*Are your eyes all red?*– and I laugh to myself because now on top everything she has read she thinks I'm a druggie.

I open the door but she stops me . . stands between me and the door. She's not looking at my eyes anymore . . she's not looking at me watch her with tiger eyes glowing through

160

my hair. She is looking at the floor . . her voice speaking to the rug. *–I know that I'm not your mother . .–*

–So stop trying to be!– I bark at her.

–. . I can help . . I can listen– she says.

I wonder what book she and my dad read that in . . the part about listening . . because they should get their money back . . it's bullshit.

–LEAVE ME ALONE!–

Janet steps to the side.

I walk out the door and run across the lawn . . I run out into the quiet street as the sun dips in and out behind the pine needles . . running with my shadow behind me . . running for safety.

Have You Seen Me?

Sometimes I feel like my brain has been split into two ghosts.

A good ghost and a bad one.

Sometimes I can't tell which I am. Both are pulling at me. And then . . suddenly . . I'm aware of being fully one or the other . . I know which I am . . good or bad . . for that minute I know . . but I also feel a feeling of being both at once and I know that is wrong . . because I know at those times I feel that way because the truth is I'm neither . . I'm in between.

Those are the times that I remember most . . the coming in and out of ghost shells.

That's who I am.

Benji.

I only exist during the moments in between. I only exist when I'm nothing.

Those are the times when I'm numb . . when nothing can hurt me . . when I can begin to store away everything that has happened to me from being one to the next. I can store my memories away like a warehouse full of boxes in my head.

Some I use to decorate my thoughts like the magazine pictures taped to the walls in my bedroom. Lacie is like one of those pictures . . my first bicycle is like one of those pictures . . my stuffed animals . . those are my pretty memories . . those are the ones I keep near me even as they fade.

Some boxes get taped up and put out of sight like my baby clothes that are taped up in the crawl space beneath my mother's trailer.

Some boxes get buried away even worse than that . . sealed off in a back room where the key is lost or broken.

Those are the boxes I've marked DO NOT UNPACK.

Those are the boxes where the demons live.

I was having my rabbit dream again only it was different . . no dogs . . nothing in the field except me and the tall grass swishing together in front of my rabbit eyes.

I looked for them.

Standing tall on hind legs . . but no demons were coming.

No clouds above me . . no river between one side or the other.

The orange sky a warm blanket of nuclear explosions.

The colors are like that when I wake up too . . the lantern still burning the same color orange in the corner . . soft light like a fallen piece of a star put behind glass.

I'm alone here as well . . in the shed.

I don't know it at first . . not exactly . . where I am . . but then I remember. I remember finding my way through the path as the sun went down . . remember the way the trees made it easier for me to pass by moving out of my way . . by burying their roots deep in the soil so that I wouldn't trip in the dark.

I remember my fingers turning the combination on the lock the way I've seen Sean do it . . remembering the numbers he would stop on like snapshots in my head.

I remember falling asleep and I remember that I was afraid to blow out the flame . . of being alone in the dark.

At least it's not cold . . not like the nights in winter that I spent in the woods by my mom's house this year. At least here there's a roof . . maybe only a board or two but still more than the house that was never finished being built where Lacie and I would take turns putting our hands over each other.

That place wasn't so bad though because at least it had memories . . but this place is better . . for tonight I guess anyplace in the world is better than the place that is supposed to be home.

I can't face my dad . . not with him knowing about me . . about how I see demons.

Not with my whole family thinking I'm crazy.

Maybe they're right though.

Maybe my mom was right when she told me I expect too much . . maybe I've always just thought things were supposed to be good but the world doesn't really work like that.

Maybe I just need to toughen up . . just like Roy said . . –*Stop being a baby and be a man*– . . isn't that what he would tell me all the time? Maybe it wasn't such bad advice. I mean so what about everything . . just go and get away somewhere and don't expect anything to ever work out . . start over knowing that the way the world works is that the world sucks . . become one of the living dead.

I can do that on my own. I don't need any of them to help me in getting lost.

Maybe my dream means that no one will follow me.

Maybe it was telling me this is my chance.

I'm too awake now to do anything . . and it's too dark to wander through the woods so I guess I'm stuck here for now anyway.

There is still a little bit of weed in the pipe by my head . . left over from when I got here . . from what was already in there.

I decide that it is meaningful medicine to light it.

The creek is loud tonight . . still running high from the rains last week . . still running fast over the rocks and fallen logs and I decide I need to see them. I need to watch the moon floating downstream and hope it can erase the image of swollen rabbit eyes from my memory.

I need to be able to look at it and think it's beautiful.

I need to know that the world can work in many different ways at once because with the stars out I'm beginning to think that if it only works the way that makes me sad then maybe I don't want to live in it anymore.

When We Become Angels

My school looks peaceful from the other side of the street . . by looking at it from here there is nothing to suggest everything that is going on inside . . no hint of all the shuffling of papers as the kids inside anticipate the final bell that will release them from another day of their four-year prison sentence.

I wait behind the bushes across the street . . watching . . waiting long enough until I'm sure that no one will see me . . that no teachers will happen to glance out the window and think they've caught someone cutting class . . not knowing that I've cut the whole day.

They'd call for me from the window . . come out for me if I ignored them and make me go to the office where I'd tell them they can't tell me to do anything because I don't even belong here . . I don't even go here anymore.

It's important they don't see me.

I'd miss her if I got caught and had to sit in the office as the vice principal pretended to be busy just to make me wait . . she would walk alone from class to the gym and never even know that I was here.

I wouldn't have even come close to this place if it wasn't for Rianna.

I promised her yesterday that I'd call her.

I promised her that I didn't hate her because all I did all day yesterday was pretend to. Then I didn't call . . I didn't show up for school and she must think I was lying when I made those promises.

The buses are all waiting in the parking lot . . their engines running and I can hear them across the street like an orchestra of machines ready to plow through the earth.

I am about to plow toward them . . about to run across the street once the next car passes.

I ignore the car horn as I dart over the dotted yellow line . . I ignore the angry shout from the car window as I'm safely on the other side because it's all bullshit since I saw the car coming and knew it wasn't anywhere near enough to hit me and that the driver is just some asshole who is angry at everything.

The bell is still sounding when I get up to the building.

The brick walls come to life with an eruption of voices that have been forced to remain mostly quiet for forty-minute periods throughout the day but now are free from the scheduled silences.

I'm able to move around the outside without having to fight the crowds that swell through the doorways inside.

I'm easily able to get to the spot where she will be . . to lean against the wall where she won't be expecting me though I've met her there every day for almost two weeks.

People start to file out . . I watch their feet . . watching for a pair of jeans with threads trailing behind them . . for the strings of a sweatshirt wrapped around small hands. I count them as they pass . . count them by twos and fours and my heart beats faster as the number gets higher because I know she is getting closer to me. But then when I see her it's almost like I never expected it.

She is walking slowly . . her head down . . her backpack draped over one shoulder and the dead blade of grass still zipped up in the front pocket.

–*Rianna!*– I shout as she gets past me . . almost far enough away that she won't hear me because I got distracted just watching her walk.

When she turns to face me the sun is behind her.

–*You didn't call me*– she says softly as other kids pass between us . . her mouth sad and I tell her that I know . . tell her with my eyes that I'm sorry as the wind blows my hair clear of my face.

I walk toward her and she folds her hands together in front of her waist . . bringing her shoulders closer together and resting her chin against her neck as she sways side to side waiting for me.

I reach out for her hands.

It's nothing I have to think about . . it's as natural as Avery would have done only it's not like him at all because there is nothing hidden behind it . . there is no other motive except to feel the way her fingerprints feel against mine.

–I had a bad night . . day really– I say. She stops pouting and tells me it's okay.

–I didn't think I'd see you today– she says. *–It made me sad.–* I tell her it made me sad too and that's why I came now.

I don't want her to go away from me . . I don't want to walk her to the gym where she will disappear in a cloud of white powder forcing me to become Dogboy again until I see her and not be Benji.

–Rianna?– I wait for her to look at me . . wait for her to lift her head so that our eyes are facing and it feels like we are one person connected at the eyes and hands . . *–Can we go somewhere?–*

–Now?– she asks . . surprised . . looking toward the gym where other girls are already walking.

–Or not . . or later . . I don't know . .– I say . . but what I really mean is *yes* . . what I really mean is *now.*

–Never mind– I say . . it was stupid . . it was selfish to think she would.

–No . . okay– . . speaking to the sky . . speaking to the clouds instead of me . . *–Okay . . let's go now–* she says. She lets go of my right hand and holds tighter on to my left . . begins to pull me away from where we've been standing like statues and back into the hallway of the school where there are still a few people at their lockers grabbing the last of what they need before the buses pull away.

–We'll go to my house– she says as we rush through the halls. *–No one's home and I can call my mom at work and tell her I didn't feel well.–*

I let her take me wherever it is she wants to go because it's enough to just be with her.

We lie across the cushions of her family room sofa . . the afternoon sunlight hidden behind the trees that grow near the windows of her house . . our reflection on the dead television screen . . our hands nervously at our sides . . our voices quiet.

I can smell Rianna on the cushions . . in the air . . the whole house smells the way she smells but diluted . . only a hint of her in everything.

Her house is nothing like any house I've ever lived in. Everything is put away . . there are no dirty dishes lying around . . no piles of papers sitting on the coffee table . . no magazines . . no shoes around wherever you might have thrown them. Everything is clean . . everything is perfect and it makes me feel ugly.

–Do you want something to drink?–

I don't look at her . . I watch her reflection instead . .

watch her as she looks at the back of my head . . watch myself lean forward . . my hair like the dirty knotted end of a mop . . watching my eyes show through when I shake my head *no* and wonder why she would ever let anyone like me into her house.

I can see her trying to think of things to say.

I don't even try.

I shouldn't have even come here. I don't know what I thought it would do . . how I thought it would help me or her. She should be in the gym doing whatever it is she needs to do. She shouldn't be with me . . here . . living on the blank television screen.

Rianna touches my shoulder and I flinch . . a flash of lightning along my spine . . like a burning until I take a breath . . until her hand comes to a rest and she smiles so I remember she is here.

—Are you going to get in trouble for not going to practice?— I ask her. I watch her pull her legs up onto the sofa . . hugging her knees with her arms and nodding. *—I'm sorry . . I didn't mean for you . . I mean . . it's my fault.—*

—It's okay. I wanted to be with you— she says.

I smile . . because the funny thing is *I* don't want to be with me . . and I can't understand why she would . . why this girl who is so pretty . . smart . . popular . . whose house is decorated with trophies and ribbons wants to be here with me . . with someone who is broken.

179

–What about you . . are you going to get in trouble for not going to school today?–

–No . . not really.– I look down at my jeans . . the stains from the creek show around my ankles . . the grass stains on my sleeves where I tried to make a pillow with my arm between the ground and me . . *–I kind of ran away yesterday. I didn't go back.–*

I watch her reaction on the tv.

I watch her twist the string of her sweatshirt in her lap as her other hand pushes her hair away from her mouth.

–Why?– she asks the way a child would ask to hear a story . . softly . . safely . . not at all accusing.

–Because–

I can feel it all hot in my throat . . tight . . like the words have to come from so deep in a cave and they don't want to come out . . holding on until I force them to let go.

–Because I don't belong here– I say. *–Because this place is bullshit . . my dad . . his family and his house . . everything . . all of it's bullshit. School too . . fuck it.–*

The freckles on her face disappear as she moves her head into the shadow . . closer to mine. Her eyes asking mine if I'm afraid.

–What if it's the same everywhere else?–

I say that if is it can't be worse.

–Was it better before . . where you lived before?–

No. It wasn't.

But I know what she's trying to do . . and I won't let her. I won't let her convince me that here is better than anywhere.

–*What if it still isn't better . . where you go?*– her voice slow . . the way winter disappears over time.

–*Do you know how bad it is for me here? Do you understand how bad it is?*– I say . . not looking at the television for the first time . . looking at her . . letting her see the way I feel. –*I don't have anything here . . I don't have any trophies . . I don't have a home. I have this . . me . . this is me . .* – and I have to wait for the pain to go away . . wait for the cracking of my voice to stop . . –*All of this is me*– I tell her . . grabbing at my clothes . . at my hair . . –*It's not a costume . . this is how I feel . . this is what it looks like on the inside of me too.*–

But I can't really make my words explain . . I can't make them say how I hate to see myself in the mirror . . how I can't look and ever make myself like me. I can't find the right way to tell her that I'm afraid . . I can't make her understand what it feels like to be afraid of your own reflection because it looks like a demon.

–*Is that what you think?*– she says . . and I see she's hurt . . and I didn't mean it like that . . I didn't mean it about her. –*You think it's so easy for me? Did you know . . that when you came over on Sunday . . did you know you were the first person I've had in my house since eighth grade?*–

181

–I'm sorry– I say . . I'm sorry because this is what I meant . . this is what I am . . I make beautiful things ugly.

–I'm not allowed to want anything that they don't want for me. That's why I have these trophies . . why I don't have any friends who know anything about me . . that's why I have to go to practice . . that's why my mom always tells me if I don't do well in the next competition that I'll never make the Olympics and then my whole life will be wasted . . then she reminds me how hard they work for me to get what I want. And I just want to tell her that I don't want anything.– She doesn't bother to sniff up the way she feels . . she doesn't bother to push her hair away from her mouth . . from sticking to the corners of her eyes.

–Rianna . .– I say . . but it doesn't matter because she won't look at me and I have to say I'm sorry to the back of her head. *–I'm sorry . . I didn't mean . .–*

But the current's pulling her away from me . . downstream. There are no angels in the sky . . nothing reflecting in her eyes.

–Don't be sorry– she says. *–If you want to go . . go. But I won't let you think that it's easy for everyone but you.–*

I want to tell her that I never meant what I said to her . . that I never thought it meant that much to her. But I never get the chance because when she stands up my bones feel like sawdust inside a scarecrow.

This isn't the way it's supposed to happen . . her walking

away and me not feeling alive . . the empty sound of her socks on the carpet and the empty sound of everything in my head where all I want to do is hold her and let her hold me because that is when we are angels . . when we are close together . . not when she is crying . . not when the tears don't make any sound as she begins to walk up the stairs . . waiting for me to say something . . hoping for me to say something but I only reach for the door because it doesn't matter anymore.

It's gone.

She isn't surprised to see me standing there without anything to say. She wipes her eyes but it does not erase the traces of what she's feeling.

I hold up my hand to wave but Rianna turns around . . already walking up toward her room.

I want to run up to her and make her understand just by holding her hands . . but I know I don't deserve to.

I don't deserve to see her crying.

I don't deserve to even be near her.

Outside everything feels different anyway . . outside is where I should be . . following the streaks of smoke that jets draw across the sky . . because my problems will only make her problems worse . . my problems need to be far away from her.

Run Rabbit Run

When my mother and I packed up and left my dad we only took the things right in front of our faces . . the things that were easy to grab like my favorite stuffed animal . . like the photo albums on the coffee table . . the clothes in the hampers or drawers instead of the ones in the closet.

We didn't tell anyone.

We didn't leave a note or make a phone call . . we only drove.

–We'll go back and get the rest of the stuff . . don't worry . . we'll get it later– my mom told me . . glancing over to me for a quick smile . . an everything-is-going-to-be-all-right smile before bringing her eyes back to the road . . bringing her hands back on the steering wheel so tightly I was afraid it might snap.

I knew we weren't going back for anything.

I knew she was only trying to make it feel better. She

didn't want me to cry about the toys and things that I was leaving . . she didn't want me to think about my dad and how we weren't going to see him.

I watched the trees go by outside the car window . . the pine trees growing so tall up to the sky . . passing over my reflection in the car window . . if I looked just the right way I'd be able to see myself and the trees at the same time.

Tuesday 6:03 pm

In the woods you can hear the voices of people in your memories . . the leaves play them back for you through the wind.

When I was little I used to think it was God.

I used to think that is how God talked to me . . that He talked to everyone like that . . that everyone heard Him speak like I did when I would daydream.

Now I know nobody else hears Him.

Now I know it's not God.

I know it's just ghosts and the whispering of demons. I know I'm not special enough for God to want to talk to me. I know He doesn't want me.

But I come here to listen to them anyway . . the voices . . so many of them . . everyone's voices that I know . . that I remember. Lacie's is there. My mom's. My third-grade

189

teacher's. They're all there . . even Roy's is there like an alligator waiting.

But mostly it's Rianna's voice that I'm hearing here now . . repeating all the things she said to me . . making me remember the things I said to her . . the things I didn't say.

To remember it makes me feel like one of the dead trees in the woods.

In the city there are no trees.

Burned clean away straight into downtown.

Only the office windows above my head . . the lights against the glass like electric snowflakes . . the sound of traffic louder than the sound of voices that I remember.

Maybe then God will talk to me.

Maybe then the angels will find me.

Maybe it will feel like home.

–Where you going?–

I lean into the car . . lowering my head to the window on the passenger's side . . to the empty seat there.

–Portland– I tell the guy who is leaning over the steering wheel to look at me . . looking at his rearview mirror and then at me again.

The road's not very wide here . . just one lane each direction and I'll have better luck on the highway . . but this guy stopped so it couldn't hurt to ask him.

–Um . . ah . .– he says . . rubbing the spot under his chin where he hasn't shaved . . scratching then. *–I'm not really going that far . . um . . but maybe.–*

I make my face tell him that I don't really understand what that means. Is that just a nice way of telling me to get lost . . to get my ass over to the interstate?

–Why don't you go ahead and get in the car . . maybe it's not that far after all– he says.

There is something about his face that makes it impossible for me to tell how old he is . . he doesn't look as old as my dad but he doesn't look younger either. He doesn't look like anything . . the way those WANTED sketches always look on the news . . like they could be anyone even though they don't look quite human.

I wonder if this is what Rianna meant when she talked about being scared . . there is nothing about the car that isn't like every other car . . nothing in the backseat that isn't in my dad's or Janet's. But maybe that's why . . maybe that's why I don't want to get in . . maybe the sameness is what terrifies me.

–Um . . that's okay . . I'll wait– I tell him.

I take only a half step back from the car before he stops me . . only enough for my breath to blow over the roof of the car instead of through the open window.

–No . . that's crazy. I was going most of the way anyway– he says . . trying to laugh . . to be my friend. But I can picture his eyes trying to see what I would look like sitting next to him.

My reflection looks different in the car paint . . pretty like pages in a coloring book. At least that is how I think he sees me . . the way he is looking at me the way men look at girls . . the way Roy looked at me.

–That's okay– I whisper . . biting my lower lip and trying to let the wind hide my eyes from him.

–I know it's okay . . *but really I don't mind. It'll be fun.–* I wonder what different scenes run though his mind when he says *fun.* I wonder what fun is for him . . if it would be sitting quietly and letting me stare out the window as he drives . . or if it means more . . if it means his hand on my knee as he drives . . if it means my head in his lap as he drives.

Or is it me who has those ideas?

Maybe it's just me who sees me that way . . the way I might look undressed on the empty car seat . . my legs sticking to the brown leather with his hand pushed up between my legs.

But if it's me or if it's him I can't tell . . and I fucking hate it that I can't . . I fucking hate it that I'm this way. I fucking hate it that those feelings are always there and I can't make them go away.

I start to walk away.

I don't want to go in this car.

I start to ignore the man as he shouts to me that he'll buy me something to eat . . for me to just get in the car with him and then he can help me.

Looking over my shoulder I shake my head at him.

–Hey! Aren't you a runaway?– he yells and I stop . . I wait for him to smile . . wait for him to tell me that the cops

193

will pick me up after not too long . . that I'm not allowed to be out asking for rides and I better go with him if I don't want to get into trouble.

But that doesn't scare me as much as the sound of opening his car door would . . as much as his hand on my stomach would . . touching me and telling me not to whine about it the way Roy would . . telling me *–It ain't no big fucking deal–* and warning me *–Don't go crying to your mommy about it like some fucking baby.–*

–I forgot . . I got to get something.– Knowing that I don't sound convincing but I don't give a fuck . . I just want to put some space between me and the look in his eyes.

–The fuck did you stop me for then? Fucking brat!– and his fist comes down hard against the dashboard . . his foot comes down hard from the brake onto the gas.

I ignore the car as it skids away . . the angry sound of the engine like the barking of metal dogs.

I look back once to see the taillights . . see them glowing red.

I begin to walk the other way . . my legs weak . . my hands hiding in my pockets . . walking away from the highway.

The phone feels cold pressed up to my ear . . colder than it should feel . . colder than it is outside. Because outside here it isn't that cold . . not cold enough for me to shiver the way I am.

I have my fingers crossed . . my hands hiding in my sleeves.

I don't know if I have them crossed hoping she will answer . . or if I'm hoping that no one will answer at all. Either way the sound of the phone ringing is enough to make me nervous . . enough to make me wish that maybe I'd never dialed the number to begin with.

When the ringing stops I go frozen inside.

–Hello?–

It's a child's voice . . her brother's voice.

I realize then that I don't have anything to say . . that calling was a big mistake . . that not sneaking through the trees near the entrance to the highway was a big mistake . . that those real distances that can be traveled by cars are better than the distance that can be traveled by telephone wires.

–*Hello?*– he says again.

I can hear someone in the background asking him who it is . . I can hear him say –*I don't know . . they won't answer me*– even though he is holding the phone away from him . . or holding his hand over the phone . . something to muffle his voice.

–*Hi*– I say because I don't want him to give the phone to her mother . . and I hear him come back . . listen to him say –*hello*– a third time before I ask him if Lacie is there.

–*No she's not here . .*– he says . . and then as if remembering something he has been taught he asks if he may take a message.

–*Um . . no . . that's okay.*– I mean what kind of message would I leave? –*Hey Lacie I think I've finally gone completely insane . . call you later?*–

–*Okay then . . bye.*– The phone goes dead.

–*Bye*– I whisper already with the phone away from my ear . . already in the motion of hanging it up . . knowing it's probably better that I didn't speak to her anyway. I would only have worried her . . would only have made her sit up all night wondering where I was . . wondering if she could protect me.

I used to believe she could.

I used to believe that Rianna could . . that someone could anyway. I don't know if I believe that anymore. And maybe that's what I'm scared of . . that it might be true . . that I was always meant to be weak . . that I was always meant just to be like a toy for demons . . because maybe that is who God is . . maybe He only made me to keep them busy . . made me for them.

I notice that the lights in the parking lot are turning on . . iridescent stars shining on the asphalt though the sun is still hanging in the sky like a quarter stuck halfway in a vending machine.

Staring at those streetlamps makes me remember how as I kid I used to wish I had been born an inanimate object . . how I used to stare at things like lamps or windows and wonder what it would be like if I was one of them . . stationary . . useful . . without feelings. Sometimes I think that's what death must be like . . sometimes I think that is what I want to be like.

A quick flick of my wrist and the tiny stone I picked up skips once before disappearing into the bushes at the other end of the parking lot.

I keep watching the cars pull in and out of parking spaces . . people going in and out of the store to pick up milk or bread or whatever.

I should go around to the side of the building where the cars don't drive . . where no one parks but the people who work in the stores and the delivery trucks that bring new versions of the same stuff every day. It'd be better back there . . safer . . but it seems hard to move . . seems like if enough people glance over at me with dirty looks then maybe I can turn into a statue the way boys do in stories like the ones that Polly reads. Besides . . this isn't the shopping center Janet goes to . . this isn't the one nearest my dad's house . . if they're even looking for me.

I take to counting the cars that pull in . . adding one every time one of them slows down on the road with the blinker on . . taking no notice of the faceless people who drive them . . no notice of the color or make of the car . . only the number matters . . only the number can keep me from thinking about things.

I can think in numbers then.

I can think *ONE . . TWO . . FORTY-SIX.*

That can make me numb then . . that can make the world disappear . . strip away layers . . make everything feel like a blank sheet of graph paper where every box can be filled with a number and nothing else can get in the way because there are lines to separate things.

But there's danger in that too.

There's a danger in not paying attention . . of not staying on guard . . of not looking at the details because things slip by you then.

They slip by me while I'm counting.

They slip by among all the other faces.

They were only number FIFTY-TWO to me.

They weren't their names . . they weren't Keith or Jordan or Sean . . they were as nameless as the other two kids with them . . as nameless as the hundred or so other people who passed by me into the convenience store.

–*What's going on Dogboy?*– Keith shouts . . pointing at me . . the look on his face telling me I'm out of place . . that something is strange about me sitting here doing nothing at all.

I know when I look at him that my face shows I wish I were farther away . . that my eyes are like rabbit eyes . . the instinct to run right there on the surface but too paralyzed to try.

–*Is the little doggy lost?*– Jordan teases . . his smirk showing just how fucking clever he thinks he's being . . how original . . and I want to tell him how I think I was seven years old when I first heard that one. Keith and the whole lot of them smile and laugh but I don't seem to be in the mood for smiles or laughter so I don't say anything.

I try to find Sean's face alone among them.

If I can find him maybe he might understand that I don't want to do this right now. But I don't get the chance because he is still by the car . . one of the stranger kids' cars . . or their mom's car most likely. Jordan and Keith start to walk toward me.

–At least he's got his clothes on– I hear Jordan say out of the side of his mouth . . pretending that it's private but making sure that I hear.

–Real funny– I say . . fucking asshole.

–What?– he shouts . . a sudden explosion of anger that is only pretending to be sudden because I can tell he hated me from the first time I said a word anywhere near him and that he's been waiting to get me like this. He squares up to me so that I have to either stand up or sit there with his boots near to stepping on my hands. *–It* is *fucking funny–* he says . . challenging me to disagree.

I look back over to the car . . brushing off the dirt and dust from my jeans . . straightening up . . looking for Sean and this time he catches my glance . . this time he nods in his slow-motion way and things begin to feel easier when he starts walking over toward me.

–Hey . . what're you doing here?– Sean says . . stepping in front of Keith so that we are standing more in a circle now and less like two animals facing off.

–Nothing– I say . . looking down at my feet so that I don't have to look at the pink color of their eyes.

Then Sean asks why I wasn't in school today and I shrug my shoulders and things begin to feel almost normal . . the way he tells me about getting stoned . . about driving around the back roads high as a fucking jet plane . .

knocking over trash cans and shit. It feels almost like I was there . . enough to make me smile anyway . . enough to make Keith smile and I sniff up all the nervousness and wipe my nose on my sleeve.

But it's only almost because of the way Jordan stays silent . . the way the other two kids who I've never seen before stay back like they don't want shit to do with me . . like I'm not worth bothering about because I'm just some dirty fuck sitting up at the shopping center who answers to the name of Dogboy.

–Yeah we missed you– Jordan says . . his lips curling over his teeth. *–We were all hoping to see your little dick again. Some of us missed yesterday's show.–*

Keith covers his mouth instantly and the other two guys express their sudden interest with laughter.

Only Sean stays the same.

Only Sean doesn't seem interested in laughing.

–Come on man . . knock it off– he says.

–I'm only fucking with you Dogboy– Jordan says . . punching me lightly on my arm.

I give him a grin because I just want him to go away . . because I don't want to do this now.

I let him win.

I let myself be a wimpy-ass little kid for him because I guess it doesn't fucking matter if it's for him or for someone else because that is who I seem to be . . who I must be because inside what I really want to do is pick up anything heavy and swing it at him.

–*We're going to smoke some more . . maybe steal lawn ornaments and shit if you want to come*– Sean says.

–*Yeah?*– saying it like a question . . like asking if it's cool for me to come along or if it's going to be more of the same.

–*Yeah . . it's cool*– Sean says . . looking to his right where Keith makes a face showing it's no big fucking deal . . looking to his left where Jordan makes the same face and looks over his shoulder to his friends who don't seem to give a fuck about anything.

Maybe it's best to go with them.

Maybe it would be good to get away from myself for a bit.

Maybe a medicated ride through the dark streets of Covington would be what I need to figure things out a bit.

–*All right . . sounds cool.*–

That's when the demons show themselves for real in Jordan's eyes . . that's when they come to the surface and stop hiding . . when they shed their skin. He twists the corners of his mouth up the way every demon I've ever known does before it lets venom spill over its teeth and across its tongue.

–*It'll be good to keep you around anyway . . girls like it when guys like us are friends with little faggots like you.*–

Then that laughter.

It never fucking leaves.

My arms feel so far away . . my body so far away from my mind like time folding in on itself . . because I don't feel anything when my arms wrap around his neck from the back . . when his body is tackled by mine and we both fall against the cement.

My skin feels like it's burning from underneath . . his breath burning underneath me as he pants . . yelling for me to –*GET THE FUCK OFF OF ME*– and saying *faggot* like it's my name . . like it's the name that was always meant for me and I figure that's okay because it's better than being a *wimpy-ass little kid* . . it's better to be feeling the way the bones in my fist feel punching his ear.

It's only a few seconds before I feel the rest of them tangle me up . . finding places to hook on to my elbows and my knees and pull at me.

It doesn't feel like anything when he punches me back.

It doesn't feel the way it did when Roy would punch me.

It doesn't feel like nothing because it doesn't matter at all either way . . because I don't matter either way . . nothing matters . . because I'm fucking nothing and you can't hurt nothing when you punch it.

I don't care at all when they call me names as they hit me. I don't care at all when they throw me against the bricks of the wall and leave me there to fall down onto my knees because I know that this is what I'm meant for . . that this is what the demons have always done me for and that I've already been damaged enough that I don't think I can break anymore.

–*Faggot*– Jordan says as he wipes the drop or two of blood from where his lip scratched up like the sidewalk was sandpaper.

–*Fuck you*– I say as I wipe the blood from where his bones made my nose bleed.

Sean comes near me . . asks me if I'm okay but I ignore him.

–*Better watch yourself*– one of the two faceless kids says to me . . pointing . . warning me to behave . . to remember my place as a big nothing piece of shit.

And I don't mind the pain so much when all of them but Sean walk away because there is so much of it that it's almost the same as feeling numb.

No Disguises

The store was pretty much on the way home no matter from where. It didn't take long to find it after my mom and I moved. It didn't take long for us to go there regularly . . my mom and I picking up bottles of brown liquid the way other moms picked up milk at the store with their kids.

–*It's my two favorite girls*– the old man behind the counter said the one time after we became the littlest bit familiar.

I went to say something.

–*I'M NOT A GIRL!*–

But my mom's hand held itself firm on my back . . holding the words inside me.

–*Oh thank you*– she said . . –*but this one's more trouble than sweet if you know what I mean.*–

I watched her wink at him.

I had no idea what she meant because I had no idea why she let him think I wasn't a boy.

But that man must have known exactly what she meant because he gave us money off so that some of the bottle was for free.

We walked to the car through the rain but I didn't even hold my mom's hand the way I always did.

–Why didn't you tell him?–

I wanted her to say she was sorry so I could be mad at her . . so I could be right and she could be wrong.

But she wasn't sorry.

She grabbed my coat by the collar.

–You almost blew it. We're not made of money Benji.–

That's when she told me that no one likes to give things away free to little boys . . especially old men who drink brown liquid from gasoline bottles.

–Whenever we go in there you'd damn well better be cute.– Then she took a sip or two before turning the key to start the car . . and I knew that it wasn't really her anymore once she had a bottle in her hand . . that she'd come back to me only when it was empty again.

Sometimes she'd make me go in there by myself.

Sometimes she didn't want to show the old man who worked there what happened to her when she drank the stuff he helped us buy. She didn't want to show him that sometimes she never got dressed anymore.

–I don't want to– I would beg and then my mom would be nice . . she would tell me it was the last time . . promise

me it was the last time as her hands would be fixing my hair . . promising me that she would be fine tomorrow . . putting Vaseline on my lips and reminding me to smile at the man behind the counter.

She would push me along with her eyes if I looked back . . walking with tiny steps to the neon window . . turning back and she would say *please* with hands like she was praying.

The carpet smelled like smoke . . like cigars and candy and I would put my fingers up to my mouth and nose so that I didn't have to smell it so much.

–How's my favorite li'l girl?– the old man would say when he saw me walking toward him . . a crooked grin on his face that moved when I walked . . a bottle in my hand . . my eyes on the label . . reading each letter carefully to make sure it matched what my mom had written on my palm in ink.

–Fine– I would mumble and make sure I looked at him the way my mom showed me to just in case she was watching from the car. I would look at him with my eyelashes the way Shirley Temple did in the movie my mom showed me . . made my eyelashes go the way my mom said would make men do anything for you that you wanted them to do . . or what my mom wanted him to do . . sell brown bottles to nine-year-olds for cheaper than before.

I only wanted him to make the medicine smell wash

away from my mother's hands . . I only wanted him to make it so she didn't smell like alcohol when she tucked me in.

But he didn't do any of those things.

He only took less money than someone else would for causing all those things.

But he only did that because I let him touch me accidentally every time . . just briefly on the neck . . or shoulder . . or let his stained fingers feel the way mine felt small in his hands when he handed back change.

But always he would touch my hair . . his fingers rotten with the smell of tobacco leaves . . –*Children have such pretty hair*– he would tell me and I would swallow . . finding it hard to keep my breath and wondering if what he said was true then why did I feel so ugly.

–*Thank you*– I would say while taking the bag. But I would never look at him . . I would never look at my mom either when I got back in the car.

–Working on your fucking masterpiece?–

I don't turn around . . don't need to . . I know Sean is standing there with his shoulder leaning against the dumpster . . looking down at me where I'm curled up with my notebook as I try to write.

Sean has a way of saying things that makes whatever words he says seem like they don't matter.

–Leave me alone– I mumble because I know what he meant to say and I don't care.

–Look man . . don't worry about them . . fuck Jordan and those guys . . you know?– . . saying what he means this time . . pushing off the dumpster so that the sound of his boot hitting the side of it echoes in the hollow chamber.

–Yeah . . don't worry about them . . right– . . pretending he's given me some useful fucking advice.

He reaches into his pocket then . . takes out a half-empty

pack of cigarettes . . takes one out. –*Want one?*– he asks even as my hand is reaching toward his . . taking the cigarette . . taking the lighter.

–*Thanks.*–

Sean doesn't sit down and I don't stand up.

I pull the fire into my chest and let my lungs fill with smoke.

–*What do you write in that thing all the time?*–

It's strange because it's the first time someone besides Rianna has asked me who isn't making fun of me . . who isn't accusing me of doing something weird. I have to take another breath of the cigarette to think about my answer . . to think if I even want to answer.

–*I don't know . . I write down things that I remember sometimes*– I say.

Sean folds his legs under him as he pulls himself to the concrete . . moving the way a bird moves . . the way Rianna moves . . so easily that it almost hurts to see him because I think it is impossible to move that way and not get wounded.

–*If you remember them then why write them down?*– he asks me . . coughing out a bit of smoke.

–*I don't know . . to make sense of them I guess . . to try to understand why . . you know?*– My voice feels tight . . like it's going to crack into pieces because it feels scary to be honest with him . . not to change the subject . . not to lie the way I've always lied whenever someone tries to get close to me.

—Does it help?—

I shake my head a little . . try to laugh a little . . *—I don't know . . sometimes it feels like it does.—* Then I put the notebook back in my backpack but without trying to be careful . . without trying to keep the pages from tearing because I probably would tear those pages out if Sean wasn't here with me.

I'm starting to feel now where Jordan hit me . . starting to feel the pain shooting through my forehead up from my nose . . like electricity . . like touching an electric socket when the charge is strong and the current runs through your veins instead of blood.

I put my hand up to my face and try to pinch the corners of my eyes to make it go away.

—Does it hurt?— Sean asks but I don't have to answer . . he doesn't even expect me to answer. *—Sorry about them . . I didn't know . . or . . I guess I didn't think. —*

I wave my hand at the air . . letting him know that it doesn't matter . . the only thing that matters is that he didn't leave with them. Why though? *—Why didn't you leave with them?—* I ask.

—I don't know.— He looks down at his hands so I can see

213

the shaved white parts of his skull outlined by his hair that looks drawn on with magic marker. *–I don't like them that much . . not even Keith really–* he tells me.

I look at him from the corner of my eyes . . sideways so that he knows that I don't necessarily believe him . . and Sean catches me . . the dark center of his eyes catches the meaning of how I'm looking at him and he puts his hands under his legs and for the first time since I met him he doesn't seem older than me . . he doesn't seem so much stronger than me . . he seems more like a boy . . more like me.

–Look man . . I only hung out with them . . you know . . because I didn't have any other friends before you came. I mean . . look at me . . not exactly a crowd of people lining up to talk to someone like me.– I look at him . . the black of his eyes matching the black of his hair . . matching the black uniform like an angel of death . . but with military boots laced above his calves. Then he looks away from me and starts to cough again . . coughing longer than I know he needs to because I know he's only trying to shake off what he's said.

–I know . . I know what you mean– . . and I don't need to say anything more than that because we understand each other . . we understand that we are rejects and that we have to stick together.

–What're you doing . . now? Going home?– he says.

I shake my head.

I hadn't thought about it . . about how I still didn't know what the hell to do or where to go. But somehow it doesn't feel so bad anymore because what I do know is that I'm not sitting here alone . . that it feels different now and doesn't seem as important what I choose to do.

—*Wanna come to my house?*— he says . . knowing that his house isn't so far from here. We can walk there . . be there in half an hour. And if I'm there . . I don't have to think about anything . . about where I've been or where I'm gonna go.

—*That sounds okay*— I say . . breathing the last breath of my cigarette before stepping it out under my heel . . before standing up with the help of the dumpster . . before walking away from the shaky light of the shopping center with my friend.

−Sean! Open the door Sean.−

His mother's hand is on the doorknob . . twisting it . . pushing on the lock that doesn't move quite the way she wants it to.

−Shit!− Sean says because I told him when we walked over here about how I ran away yesterday. That's why we came in the house through his bedroom window . . that's why we had the stereo on louder than usual so that no one would hear two voices coming from the back room of the house.

−Sean I mean it . . open the door!−

I look at Sean and he looks at me . . asking me what he should do. I shrug my shoulders. I mean what the hell can he do really . . it's not like we can barricade the door with his dresser and pretend that nothing is out of the ordinary.

–Hide– Sean whispers like we're in some kind of movie and I'm at the end of the line.

–Where?– I ask in a tone that lets him know that I have no intention of hiding . . of crawling under his bed or into his closet while his mom hunts around the room like a detective carrying a spatula instead of a gun. *–Just open the door–* I say and so it's his turn to shrug his shoulders.

–Just a second Mom– he hollers . . turns down the music and steps over to the door where he switches the lock over to let her hand turn free and let her head poke into the room with suspicion in her eyes.

–What are you doing in here?– . . and she starts to sniff at the air the way my dad's dog sniffs at my jeans in order to get me caught. *–Are you doing drugs?–* she asks and Sean tells her no but by then it doesn't matter because she has seen me.

–Hi Mrs. Roberts– I say.

She says hi back to me but I can see in her expression that she is thinking something else . . I can see it as clearly as I can see the moon when I lie down on my bed and look out my window at night.

She knows.

She has spoken to someone at my house and she knows.

It's okay that she knows though.

I don't care that she knows.

I guess I wouldn't have come here if I didn't sort of want someone to know.

–How long have you been in here?– she asks Sean and he says *–not long.–* She raises her eyebrows to ask him if he's sure . . trying to find out if I've been here the whole time.

–We just got here . . like an hour ago– he says . . raising his voice at not being trusted.

But his mother isn't listening anymore because she is beginning to notice the swelling under my eyes from across the room . . noticing it more as she walks over to Sean's bed. *–What happened?–* she asks . . reaching her hand out to touch my face because for some reason touch makes everything seem more real.

I pull my head away . . *–Just got in a fight . . that's all . . it's nothing.–*

She says it doesn't look like nothing and that she'll be right back with something to put on it.

I remember when Roy hit me the same way . . when my eye was almost swollen shut and the skin around it all bruised. I remember telling my mom the same thing . . *–It's nothing–* . . and I remember her telling me that *–damn right it's nothing–* and that if I didn't go running my mouth off all the time at Roy then he wouldn't have to be so strict.

–Just do what the hell he tells ya!– she yelled . . punctu-

ating it with broken glass on the countertop and the sound of her bare feet heading back into the dark cave of her bedroom.

I remember thinking that if she only knew the things he told me to do . . then she would be on my side. But I'm not so sure anymore . . not so sure she didn't know . . not so sure it isn't exactly the same thing as with the man at the liquor store . . because I'm starting to realize that the only thing she ever wanted me for was to make it easier for her to get what she needed . . that she could let them all use me so that she could use them.

—I think my mom knows— Sean says.

—I know she does— I say.

—Do you want to go? We can get out the window again.—

I tell him it's okay . . that I don't want to go anywhere.

I think he's about to tell me that I'm crazy when his mom comes back in the room with a towel wrapped around ice and a tube of smelly cream that she wipes around my eyes and on the scratches across my cheek.

She doesn't say anything as she does this . . the way a nurse would . . silently . . treating the wound and not the patient. *—Keep that ice on your face until it melts . . it'll feel better soon—* she says and I smile and tell her thank you.

Then she leaves the room . . keeping the door open.

Sean and I look at each other . . both knowing where

she's going . . the sound of her slippers disappearing near the kitchen where their phone hangs on the wall. We both know what number she's dialing.

–*Sorry about this . .*– Sean says. I tell him it's not his fault. Then we sit there and wait and I can't help thinking that it's like being sent to the principal's office . . waiting with the secretary with the principal's door closed . . waiting to be called in there and not knowing if what you've done is considered serious or just a minor misunderstanding. I don't know how my dad is going to see it . . I won't know until Sean's mom comes back in the room . . and then she won't even need to speak . . I will know from the look on her face which way he's decided.

Only I don't get to figure it out that way because Sean's mom doesn't come back to his room . . she calls for him instead.

Sean looks over at me nervously before getting up to leave the room . . I cross my fingers in my pocket and try to make it seem like I'm not worried . . that I don't care . . that I'm tougher than I am.

The ice starts to make my skin feel tight . . starts to make the stars in my head twinkle and die out one by one so that I can concentrate on trying to hear their words from the other side of the house.

But I can't understand what is being said so I lie

down . . falling backward and letting the blanket bunched up behind me catch my fall.

With my eyes closed it's easy to think about everything that has gone wrong . . how bad I screwed everything up with Rianna . . how much Jordan and Keith and everyone they know except Sean is going to hate me now. It's easy to think about the car too . . how near it was to me . . how easy it would have been to open the door . . to sit next to the man who wanted me to sit next to him.

I wonder where I'd be now if I'd gotten into that car. Maybe I'd be in Portland . . downtown where the stores would be getting ready to close . . searching the side streets for a place that didn't look so open where I could curl up and close my eyes like I am now.

But then I think how maybe I wouldn't have made it much farther than I am now . . maybe I would have ended up wherever that man lived . . lying on his bed instead of Sean's and knowing that I probably would've let him do anything he wanted to do . . that I would have done as I was told . . that I wouldn't have put up anywhere near as much of a fight as I put up with Jordan . . that I would have pulled off my clothes for him like I did for Roy . . and that's when I know that going away wouldn't make anything better . . that Rianna is right . . that those things that frighten me are with me no matter where I am because they are not attached to places . . they are attached to me.

–*She called your parents*– Sean says as he walks back into the room . . dragging his feet . . head down because he feels that maybe it's his fault since she's his mom.

–*I figured*– . . lifting only my head up from the blanket.
–*Are they on their way to pick me up?*–

Sean shakes his head.

–*They say it's okay for you to stay here tonight if you don't want to come home*– he says . . says it's okay with his mom too as long as I let her drop me off there in the morning.

I thought my dad would have been halfway out the door the second Sean's mother mentioned my name . . I thought he'd be here pushing his way into Sean's room if only to pull me out by my hair.

I guess I hadn't thought much of him.

–*Is that cool?*– Sean asks because he needs to go back and tell his mother one way or the other.

I ask him if we can turn the stereo on again . . hoping that music will keep me from thinking at least until tomorrow morning . . hoping that we can listen to every single album that Sean has . . hoping that he can finish telling me the stories behind every one of them and how his brother let him keep them on the condition that Sean doesn't try to change the way they're organized by mood . . that he doesn't get rid of any of them . . even the ones on the list

222

that his brother has made entitled TO BE DESTROYED AFTER I DIE because he thinks those albums are total shit but for the sake of the collection he said he has to keep them.

   –*Sure*– Sean says.

   –*Then yeah . . it's cool.*–

Speaking in Silence

Both cars are in the driveway when neither should be.
Both cars should be at work.

Both Janet and my dad should be at work and I should
be at school but none of us are where we are supposed to be
since all three of us are sitting around the kitchen table.

There was the *how are you doing* and *what happened to
your eye?* the instant I came in the door. I answered by
shrugging.

No one knows what to say anymore so we all spend a lot
of time clearing our throats and not saying anything. Not
even the dog wants to interrupt the silence by barking or
begging . . he sits there on the tile . . watching us . . knowing that our faces are considering our words carefully
because every syllable is serious.

–*Where's Polly?*– I ask because I can't stand them looking at me and because I can't think of anything else to say

227

since I'm staring at her empty chair at the table instead of staring at them.

–She's at school– Janet says. It's a polite answer to a polite question.

–Where I should be . . right?– . . looking over at my dad for the first time since I walked in the door. I know that's what he's thinking . . I know that's what he wanted to say when he bit his lip and let Janet answer the polite way.

–Benji . . don't– he says . . shaking his head . . breathing loudly through his nose as his face begins to get red.

–Don't what?– I ask . . defying the look he gives me . . knowing damn well what he means and not giving a shit really if he does or doesn't get angry because he has no right either way because this isn't about him.

–Don't get me agitated!– he shouts. I can feel my eyes begin to glow . . begin to feel the jungle closing around me . . begin to feel the need to defend myself from demons through hiding.

–Both of you . . knock it off– Janet says. *–I'm not going to sit here and let the two of you yell and scream and hate each other!–* Then she takes a deep breath and waits for my dad and me to stop staring each other down like enemies do in war movies. *–That's what got us like this in the first place . . can't we try to have a little understanding?–* . . and then she backs off from the table . . lifting her elbows off the table and pushing her chair away.

I know it's because she's upset . . not upset the way my dad is . . upset like she's going to cry and so instead she goes over to the sink and asks us if either of us would like something to drink.

—I tried to talk to him the other day Janet . . he didn't want to— my dad says . . making a case . . playing the lawyer and letting Janet play the judge. I guess that makes me the defendant.

—So it's my fault? I guess everything is my fault!— I yell.

My dad doesn't get any of his words out . . the words that are burning right under his skin . . he doesn't get them out because Janet throws her glass down in the sink . . getting out just one word . . *—ENOUGH!—*

The dog slowly backs away from under her feet . . slowly sliding out of the room.

—It's no one's fault . . okay?— she tells us . . both of us . . *—Or it's all of our faults . . mine too . . for reading your diaries . . and yours for running off . . and yours too for not listening even when nothing was being said.—*

There is a pause where we all catch our breath . . the amount of time it takes for Janet to take her seat again . . the amount of time it takes for each of us to remember every minute of what life has been like since my dad picked me up at the bus station weeks and weeks and weeks ago.

—It doesn't matter whose fault it is— she says . . putting her hands across the table for my dad's . . *—What matters is*

229

that we fix whatever is wrong . . that's what families do.–
Then she reaches for my hand but I pull it away because no
matter how good what she's saying to me sounds I'm still
not convinced it's not just more bullshit.

My dad begins to wipe at his mouth with his hand . . rubbing at his chin . . at the places where he shaved earlier this
morning . . breathing loudly through his nose again but trying to keep it inside him more . . trying to hear what Janet
is saying even though I know his habits and know that he
isn't any less pissed off than he was the second Sean's mom
dropped me off.

–Benji I don't know what to do. I've tried . . I have– he
says and I wish he would make a list of what he's tried so
that I could see it . . so that he could see it and see that it's
a pretty short fucking list.

It's easy then to let my habits take over too . . easy to
let my hair fall around the angles of my face and easy to bring
my eyes away from him and toward the floor.

*–Maybe . . maybe you want me to call your mom.
Maybe you want to go back there?–* and it doesn't even
sound like it's that hard for him to say . . that they are words
he's had on his tongue from before I even showed up to
live here.

I start the screaming even before the words come out
because that is exactly what I mean about him not trying . . that he doesn't even have any fucking clue what it's

like for me . . how hard it was for me to call him . . to come here . . how completely fucking awful it must have been to make me want to ask him for a favor.

–*You want to dump me back there? You want to get rid of me now too!*– . . and maybe I would've been better off in that car . . even if I ended up dead maybe I'd have been better off because at least then I wouldn't have to know that I was right . . that no one does want me after all.

–*NO DAMMIT! NO ONE IS TRYING TO GET RID OF YOU . . I JUST DON'T KNOW WHAT IT IS YOU WANT FROM ME!*– his fist pounding on the table and now there is nothing Janet can do to keep us from getting at each other . . from using our voices like weapons.

–*I DON'T WANT ANYTHING . . OKAY? . . I DON'T WANT ANYTHING!*–

But it just sounds like noise in my head . . like the noise of dogs chasing me with fire in their tails and teeth marks on my bones . . like thunder that roars but then fades . . and everything goes silent after that . . everything is quiet after the noise.

–*That's not what I meant*– my dad says . . shaking his head . . that look on his face . . the same look as when I used to tell him I didn't want to go to practice or that I didn't want to sign up for baseball . . that look that is meant to tell me I'm a pain in the ass . . that I purposely make things difficult . . *just like my mother* . . that's how he used to put

231

it . . that I was just like her and both of us had no other purpose except to make his life harder.

–*What did you mean then? Huh?*– Because I want to hear him say it . . I want to hear him say again that I'm like her . . because then I'll know he never gave a shit about me . . because then I can tell him what she's really like . . the way she lives life like she's already dead . . the way she is a home for demons . . the way that it's his fucking fault because he was never there to chase them away . . he was never there to keep me safe.

But then he breathes through his mouth again . . a deep breath before facing the window . . his eyes far away . . his eyes looking past the trees that grow there and looking into somewhere else that I can't see.

–*I just . . I don't want for us to fight anymore*– he says.

And maybe because it's not what I expected him to say or maybe because I finally realize that I blame him for everything that is wrong . . or maybe it doesn't even matter why I'm crying . . just that I am.

–*Can we please . . can we just not fight anymore?*– he says . . and I don't know what to answer so I don't answer anything . . and I guess that is sort of like not fighting . . or maybe it isn't because maybe I'm quiet only because I'm choking back tears since I don't want to let him hear me cry because hearing someone cry is different from seeing them cry.

I know I have to leave the room . . that I don't want him

or her to say another thing to me. So I get up from the table . . not looking either of them in the face . . doing my best to keep from covering my face with my hands . . doing my best to keep it all inside for a few more seconds until I get into my room with the door safely locked and my head safely buried in my pillow.

I push past my dad when he starts to stand up to stop me.

But he doesn't even try that hard . . he doesn't even need Janet to tell him to let me go this time and I guess that means he's starting to understand me a little bit . . understanding that sometimes I need to be alone in order to let someone get close to me.

I've always liked the rain because it covers over everything whereas the sun only exposes the parts of the world you don't want to see. The colors even look better in the rain . . the same way drawings can look better than photographs.

It's raining now.

It's been raining outside my bedroom window for the past few hours. The puddles are growing larger . . meeting up with each other . . becoming little ponds and lakes. I'd like to think my dad and I could become like that. I'd like to think that this morning around the table we were all like puddles . . separate . . but if we let more of ourselves out then maybe we could be like the rain as it collects outside my window.

If I told my dad that he'd probably roll his eyes.

He would tell me –*That's not how men deal with things*– because he believes what those old-fashioned shows believe . . he believes in being tough . . he doesn't believe in feelings . . he doesn't believe in things that can't be seen.

Even when I was little he used to tell me I was too *sensitive* about things. And I wonder if he thought I couldn't tell . . that I didn't catch the looks he gave my mother . . that I didn't hear the whispered phrases he spoke when he thought I was out of his hearing.

But I did catch them.

I did hear them.

And I've held them inside me my whole life. But this morning he asked me to let go of them . . to stop hiding them from him and show him who I really am. Only I'm not so sure he really wants to see who I am on the inside or if he wants me to show him something more simple . . something he wants to believe is there . . something that will make him feel better.

Outside the grass is coming through the ground thicker as spring grows older. Memories are like those shoots of grass . . popping up so fast that you can never keep track of them all. But some of them grow taller . . some of them stand above the others and you can see them clearly because they are not like the others . . they have grown into weeds with bushy flowers that are not at all like looking at garden flowers because these are ugly . . these are ones that you want to pick and discard . . but they keep growing back faster than you can keep up with them.

My fifth birthday is one of those memories . . one that doesn't go away . . one that grows back every time my dad asks me to be honest with him.

I wanted a dollhouse . . the one I saw in the store flyer that came as part of the newspaper. I wanted it because it looked like our house but because the furniture was different and because the people who came with it didn't look at all like our family.

I wanted it because the picture made it look like the people wanted me to make up stories for them . . wanted me to make them alive for them.

–This one . . this is the one I want– . . pointing to the glossy pages and not caring that the ink from the ad would stain my fingers . . showing it to my mother so that she would make sure to get the right one and not just one that looked like it.

My mom smiled.

I can remember that so clearly because her smile has become only a memory . . having a mother has become only a memory and I let those grow taller so that I don't lose them.

–You'll have to ask your father– she said. She always

said that because my father believed in making decisions for everybody.

I never liked when she would say that though.

I never liked asking him for anything.

Because he always wanted a reason . . he always wanted to know *why* . . he could never say yes just because it might make someone else happy.

My dad looked over at me . . his feet on the coffee table . . the newspaper in his lap. –*What?*– he asked . . moving aside his paper and putting his arm up high so that I would come over to him . . next to him.

I stood perfectly still.

–*Come on . . show me*– he said . . trying to copy my mother's smile but I knew it wasn't the same . . I knew his was only there because that is what my mother expected from him.

My mother had to give me a little shove to start my feet moving. I put my hand up to my mouth and let my shoulders go all shy and my father rolled his eyes at my mother the way he always did because he never understood why I would be afraid of him. But I was . . I was afraid of the way he looked at me . . I was afraid of showing him the picture and thought about pointing to a different one.

Slowly I saw him change . . saw him start to breathe through his nose . . saw him start to rub his face the same

way he always did when I would get shy around him . .
the way he still does when he loses patience with me.

I didn't sit on his lap or next to him.

I stood with my head down in front of him.

–*This one*– I mumbled and didn't really point.

–*What one . . what? This?*– . . and something about the
way his finger looked pointing to the dollhouse made me
feel like I'd done something wrong . . something about the
way he looked at me made me feel ashamed and I crossed
my arms in front of my naked stomach and turned my hips.

–*Mmmm hmmm*– I whispered into my palm and he
looked again at the picture.

He told me –*That's not for you*– and then he put the
flyer down beside him where I was supposed to sit and
picked up his newspaper again.

I wanted to say –*But that's what I want*– but my mother
shook her head . . gave me her secret sign of when to let
it go.

I didn't get the dollhouse I wanted for my birthday.

I got a dollhouse for boys.

The house wasn't really a house at all. It had windows
and a door but it had bullet holes in it too . . and a jail . .
and a command center.

The people weren't really people either. They all wore
green and had names like general and corporal and soldier.

My dad wouldn't understand if I told him this memory.

He would remind me that I played with those army men for hours and hours and for years to come. And it's not that he's wrong . . it's not that I didn't . . or that it wasn't one of my favorite toys . . because it was. It's not about any of that.

It's about the way I remember more how I felt standing in front of him than I remember the toy . . how cold it felt wearing only my underwear even though it felt warm seconds before . . how it felt like his eyes were looking down to see if he could tell if I was still a boy or not . . how that is the memory I had when Roy stood there smiling at me . . how ashamed I felt for being me.

And now my dad is sitting in a new living room . . reading another paper . . but still waiting for me to come in there and ask for that dollhouse all over again. Because this is the same thing . . this is me having to tell him things that I know I don't want to and having to trust that he doesn't come back again with a plastic bag filled with army men and a toy base made to look like it has been attacked even when it's brand-new.

And I can't.

I can't trust him that way.

That is what has kept us puddles . . that is what keeps us from being ponds.

Nothing

Nothing happened today.

I didn't go to school because both Janet and my dad think I should take some time off.

I didn't leave my room today except to eat.

I didn't speak except to say please or thank you.

I drew a picture of myself in my notebook wearing a Native American headdress because I thought maybe it would make me feel brave the way Lacie drew pictures of herself as an angel.

But I didn't look brave.

I tore it up because I looked young and weak.

I tore it up so it's like I never drew it.

So that it's like today never happened.

Secrets Never Last Forever

I told her to go away but Janet insists on me letting her in my room. I told her to tell whoever was on the phone for me that I was sleeping or in the shower or anything that would get them to hang up but she says it's not good for me to stay shut in like this and that it might not be a bad idea to talk to my friends.

I want to tell her that talking over the phone is the same thing as talking to ghosts because you can't see them . . that it's really not talking at all and therefore she should just leave me alone.

But Janet won't do that.

They won't leave me alone at all.

At least one of them has been in the house nonstop since I came back . . guarding me . . making sure I don't run away again or do something worse.

–*FINE!*– I open the door so she can thrust the new

wireless phone into my room. When I won't take it from her hand she places it on the carpet and closes the door again . . softly . . sealing in the quiet so that I can hear the voice on the other end repeating my name like a question . . *–Benji? Benji?–*

I wonder how long she will repeat my name . . if I never put my hands on it to pick it up . . if I never let her hear me breathe . . how long will she say *Benji* into the dead air?

–It's me . . Lacie.–

I stop wondering then.

I know she would say my name forever . . not caring that I answer or not . . only caring that I can hear her . . only caring that the sound of her voice is like an angel's to me.

I sit down on the floor near the phone.

I will not be a monster to her.

I will not let myself treat her the way people sometimes treat me with their passing looks in the hallway or in the classroom or sitting on the curb.

I won't let her feel worthless.

–Hi– I whisper.

My voice sounds strange . . out of practice.

–Hi– she says . . and I can feel the smile in her voice . . I can feel the way her cheeks get warm and it makes me feel different too . . knowing that I can make that happen even being so far away.

–I'm sorry . . about the last time I called you . . I was just . . it's just that . . things are kind of weird for me right now.– I can feel my voice getting clearer as the light fades in my room and the sun begins to set . . the sky turning a deep blue like the deepest part of the ocean . . and I notice that talking to her over the phone is not at all like talking to a ghost . . it's comfortable . . safe.

–I thought maybe you were mad at me– she says.

–No– I've never been mad at her . . I could never.

–Oh . . because you seemed like it . . like maybe I did something wrong– . . and I can tell by the way the last part is slurred that she has put her fingers on her tongue.

I bring my hand close to my mouth and pretend to be like her.

It makes her feel near . . doesn't make me feel like she's gone . . that she's not so far from here.

–You didn't do anything . . – I say . . bringing my knees together and bringing them close to me . . holding them the way Rianna does because now I have to think of her . . because she's here too . . I can feel her here too. And it's all so confusing that I don't know what to say . . because I don't know what any of us are supposed to be . . boyfriend and girlfriend . . or friends . . or if there is even a difference between them.

–There's this girl– . . whispering softer now . . *–and*

that's why I was like that . . I'm sorry– and it hurts so much to say . . hurts so much to be honest . . but I'm hoping the hurt gets better after a time . . after I stop lying.

–. . oh . .– she says . . and the letters are so small . . the sound of it is the sound of the smallest word . . I wonder how it can get inside the center of my bones and affect me the way it does.

I can hear her little brother in the background . . I can hear him say her name twice . . his voice above her head so I know where in the house she is . . I can tell he's at the top of the stairs . . I can tell she's two steps from the top with her back leaning against the wall the same as I am. *–Malky in a minute . . okay?–* she says holding the phone away and he tells her *–but I'm hungry now–* before shuffling away.

Then I hear her catch her breath as I catch mine.

I wait for her to speak . . but she doesn't say anything and I'm afraid that's worse.

–Do you hate me?– I ask.

She doesn't answer but the silence has the same effect.

–I'm sorry.– I know I've said it already but I need to say it again . . a thousand times again . . I need to because I know what the silence is doing to her . . I know her smile is gone . . her eyes are darker than they were only a minute ago when I said hi.

–I know I fuck everything up– . . saying it to myself as much as to her. *–Lacie? I didn't mean to . . I didn't want . .–*

but I don't know what it is I'm trying to say so I leave it that way . . unfinished.

–*Do you like her?*–

Lacie's voice sounds like a ghost's voice now . . like ghosts living inside her have found a way out . . found a way to travel this far into my room to say what they have to say before disbanding.

–*Do you like her a lot?*–

I think about the way Rianna looked in the park last Sunday . . the way she looked lying on the ground . . the way I must have looked lying next to her . . against her.

I think about the way I hurt her the other day . . the way she looked at me . . the way her eyes had as much pain as mine.

Then I think about the letters that Lacie wrote me . . how I could tell even by the way she drew each letter that she was happier . . and I think then maybe it is all my fault . . maybe I'm the one who causes everyone to hurt . . that by looking for angels I only bring the demons to new people the way my mother does.

–*I don't know*– I tell her.

–*It's okay if you do . . I don't hate you.*– Something about the way she speaks is so brave that I can feel my eyes getting hot . . can feel my skin itchy and red.

–*Lacie? . . It's not even that . . it's everything.*– Then my voice goes . . the sound a dog makes when it yelps . . the sound a baby makes when storms approach . . and I don't know if I can do this anymore . . if it wouldn't be better to hang up and let the shadows become a tomb where I will stop existing.

I don't know how she is able to do it . . how she is able to push aside what an asshole I am and still care about me when she says my name . . when she tries to get me back onto the phone instead of having it rest on my shoulder afraid to listen . . afraid to speak. *–What's wrong Benji?–*

–Everything– . . and again it's only one word but it means so much.

–But I thought it was better there . . aren't things better there?– she asks . . and I want to tell her she only thinks that because that's what I told her . . those are the lies I told her to hide the lies I told her about before when I lived there with my mom . . not really lies . . just not the whole truth but it's the same thing.

–No . . I mean . . not really– I say.

What I want to say is that it doesn't matter . . here or there . . that the same things are wrong . . the same problems . . that nothing ever goes away.

–What about your dad? I thought he was better than your mom– she says. I tell her that maybe he is but that still he can't understand. Then she asks about my stepmom . . asks me if maybe she would understand and I tell

252

her I don't think so but that I never thought about her that much in all of this. Lacie tells me how she and her mom have become like friends . . how all the memories I have of her talking to me about her mother aren't really true anymore . . how she does understand even when we thought she could never.

I tell her that even when I write my secrets down I only end up tearing them to pieces . . and I could never speak them because I could never tear up what I've said in the same way and therefore I don't think I could ever tell anyone.

–You could tell me . . maybe not now . . but whenever you want to because no matter what we'll always be friends . . right?–

In my room the sun has completely died . . the night has taken over the sky the way colors on a map change when a country is taken over in war . . but the feeling is different than that . . different than night . . than darkness . . because even in the darkness angels exist.

I stopped believing in things as a kid because there was never any proof . . nothing I could see. I stopped believing in Santa Claus and the Tooth Fairy and God. I started believing only in demons because they don't make it hard for you to see them . . they don't hide away like those who are good.

I was beginning to think angels were the same way.

I was beginning to think I made them up too.

But now I have proof . . Lacie is proof . . because only an angel could still say that to me after what I said to her.

–*Thanks Lacie.*–

And if she can be an angel maybe others can be too . . maybe not everything has to be as bad as I let myself believe sometimes . . maybe all I have to do is trust a little . . believe in some good in some people a little.

I've thought about what I'm going to say so many times that when I rehearse the words again in my head they no longer make any sense. I get nervous that they won't make any sense when I say them out loud either and that maybe I should wait until morning because I hear the television switch off in the living room . . hear footsteps back and forth from the bathroom to the kitchen . . traveling the routine they always travel before getting ready for bed.

But I also know that if I don't say them now I will never say them.

I know I have to be brave . . that if Lacie could be that brave with me then I have to be brave too if I'm ever going to make it up to her.

The footsteps pass by my room again.

I know they will not be passing by another time and that I have to get off my bed . . that I have to clear my throat . . that

255

I have to try to forget what I rehearsed and just say what I feel. And even though I know it's what I have to do it still doesn't keep my entire body from going numb . . doesn't keep my heart from pounding so hard that it's strangling me.

I open the door and am surprised that it's not any brighter there than in my room . . that there are no shadows of anyone walking past and I begin to think I might be too late. Then a light goes on again in the living room and I know that I haven't missed anything as I walk through the hallway.

I stand in the doorway waiting to be seen because I can't bring myself to speak . . not first.

–Oh . . hi. I didn't know you were still up.–

I stay close to the wall . . feeling safer being attached to it . . allowing it to hold me up. I lift my hand and push the hair away from my face . . tucking it behind my ear. *–Janet . . –* I say and wait for her to look at me . . to see that I'm not hiding . . *–Know how you read the stuff I wrote?–* . . and she puts aside all expressions . . puts aside anything that would make me stop and nods . . *–I didn't make any of it up–* I say.

She breathes deeply so that I can see the lines in her face . . the lines around her mouth and her eyes which are still faint and new but which show more when she breathes like that . . when she is searching for the right way to say things. *–Do you want to talk about it?–*

I shrug my shoulders.

I wonder if it's enough having told her only that much.

–*Whatever you want to tell me*– she says –*is okay.*–

Then she moves aside and I move toward the sofa . . move near her because somehow being close will maybe make it easier to speak.

She doesn't ask any questions . . she doesn't pretend to know everything before I tell her the way my dad would . . she doesn't roll her eyes or do anything that will make me go quiet and so it's easier for the words to come out . . for me to begin to talk without crying . . to tell her about what it feels like to be me.

I tell her about my mom first.

I tell her how I would find her sometimes in my room on the floor . . how things would be knocked over on my dresser . . how my things had been replaced with bottles that I had bought for her when we both pretended that I was pretty.

I tell her how it felt like my mother died and how it made me feel like maybe I was dead a little too since I lived with her.

Janet doesn't say anything . . she doesn't get all *concerned* or tell me that it's all in my head the way I was afraid she might . . the way I was afraid anyone I told might. Instead she stays quiet so that I can continue.

And I do. I tell her everything . . even the things that weren't written down.

I tell her about Lacie.

I tell her about Rianna.

I tell her how I wish I could make them into one person with all the parts that I like about each of them.

I tell her about Sean and Jordan and what happened at the empty shopping center before I came home that day and found her with my notebooks.

Then I tell her about Roy.

And even just saying it out loud makes me feel scared . . makes me look over in the corner to make sure he's not standing there . . that the demons aren't standing there . . that their faces don't show in the pattern of the wallpaper . . pointing and laughing at me.

When I don't see them there . . I start to cry.

When I don't have anything left to say I can only make sounds come out of my mouth instead of words because I'm not yet empty inside . . there is still hurt inside that needs a sound.

But then I start to hear Janet's voice over the noise I make . . somewhere just above me like birds that fly low in the sky. *–It's okay now . . you're okay–* and then I start to feel her arms around me even though I'm sure they have been there for a while and it was just that I couldn't feel them until I got everything out.

I don't know how long it is that we sit there like that.

I don't know how long it is before I stop shivering . .

before a sense of calm comes over me. I don't know exactly when the tears stop . . only that they have because my eyes are closed. I don't know how many times she touched my head and whispered *–okay–* because when I fall asleep I can still feel her there . . can still feel her words in the air.

Different in the Morning

The sun is so strong that the blue around its edges has been bleached white . . the whiteness spreading . . the blueness disappearing as the sun burns away at it like a spark in the center of a blanket. It's going to be the first day that spring starts to turn to summer instead of being just the milder end of winter.

The trees show it too . . the flowers already turned to leaves that reach up to get their share of the heat eating away at the clouds . . the branches full and green the way children draw them.

I spread my arms to try to feel some of what they must feel. I don't care what it is that I hope to feel . . anything but the emptiness that is sitting there in the pit of my stomach . . in that place where I've kept my secrets for so long . . locked up . . layer upon layer covering it over like the dirt over a grave but all that soil has been shifted.

263

If I stand still long enough maybe the sun can burn through the shell that covers me . . maybe it can burn through to let me free because I've been nothing but a shield for my secrets for so long . . without them to protect I have no purpose . . a safe with nothing stored in it.

But I'm sick of letting them define me.

I'm sick of being whatever it is they think I am.

It's my fault . . I've let myself be nothing for so long that any name that anyone called me would attach itself. I would be whatever they wanted as long as what was inside me stayed safe. I'd be Roy's *wimpy-ass little kid* . . Jordan's *faggot* . . the teachers' *freak* . . didn't matter because I thought it was better to be those things than to be me.

Fuck them.

I'll be me from now on.

I'm not going to be silent.

I'm going to let it all out and let them hear it and if they don't like what they hear that's not my problem. If it makes them uncomfortable . . if it makes them angry . . if it means I have to fight and kick and scream then I will.

That's what it means not to be damaged.

That's what it means to be alive.

I want to be alive again. I don't want to be dead . . I don't want to hide away in the shadows.

When I walk out of my house this morning it's because I don't want to face anyone . . not Janet . . not my dad who must know everything by now. I don't want to see my reflection in their eyes because I'm afraid what will be there . . what I will look like . . what the real me will look like.

I was going to lock myself in the shed down by the creek . . I was going to let the woods separate me from the rest of the world . . but then I stop. I spread my arms out to feel the warmth the sun has . . its rays reaching all the way down to me . . inside me . . lighting up what has been dark for so long and the only thing left to do is scream.

I scream so loud that the whole world is forced to hear me.

I scream so long that even the birds that at first flew away have come back and grown used to me.

I scream so forcefully that I can feel the demons retreating because the sound that is coming out of me is telling them to find someone else to torture because I'm stronger than they thought . . and I don't care who sees me and I don't care what the fuck they think of me because I have a right to be here . . I have a right to be alive.

I drag my arm against the lockers as I walk . . amazed at the echo in the halls where the fragments of a million conversations usually serve to drown out every thought . . amazed at the freedom to zigzag from one side to the other . . always with my arm outstretched . . with my hand bouncing off each locker and letting my feet fall in line with the clanking rhythm of the hollow sound it makes.

There's something not right about a school building on the weekend. The banners advertising school spirit have no meaning without anyone to read them . . the desks have no purpose without anyone to sit in them . . the classrooms useless with the lights off and the doors locked . . the halls like veins without any blood cells running through them.

I know this building doesn't look at me as its lifeline. I'm not part of the circulation that creates what it is . . that forms its opinions or trends or whatever it is that high school is supposed to be about. I'm only in its breeze . . allowed to move through with the rest of the students as long as I don't cause too big a disturbance.

I think it will get used to me though.

It'll have to . . because I'm not going anywhere . . and I'm not taking my hand away from these lockers to stop the noise that it's making. I'm not going to be kept in back rows and silenced when the enforcers try to push me around.

I'm not saying it's going to be easy.

I'm not saying there won't be assholes who try to stop me . . who try to force me back into the shadows . . I'm just saying that if there are consider this fair fucking warning!

And it's not going to take long for it to start . . for me to prove myself right because a man comes around the corner at the end of this hall.

–*Excuse me . . where you headed son?*– he asks.

I notice the look on his face isn't quite how I would have thought . . not a look that can get to me . . a look more like he's afraid of me . . and I guess there's a power in being misunderstood . . that maybe not everyone has the control over me that I always thought they did.

–*I'm going to watch the gymnastics team*– I say . . never slowing down . . never for a second acting like I'm not going to continue right on past him.

–*Who gave you permission?*– . . and already his voice doesn't have the authority it had when I was farther away.

–No one . . why? . . I need permission just to watch?–

I put my hands on the gym door . . ready to push it open . . giving him one last second to say something but he just shakes his head . . *–Guess not–* he mumbles.

Walking through the doors is like walking into a new life . . one where anything is possible . . where I have control of what will happen. The sounds the athletes make . . the chalk storm that gets caught up in the air . . the glances of the people near the door . . all of them are tools that I can use . . it is all only suggestions of what might be and I can use them any way I want . . can make of them whatever I want because for the first time since I can remember there is no trace of demons in any of them.

For right now I choose to ignore them.

I choose not to respond to the handful of parents already sitting on the bleachers . . or to the assistant coaches who look to me as a distraction . . or even the whispers of some of the girls who are waiting their turn on this or that piece of equipment. I'm not here for any of them . . I'm here for her . . I'm here to watch her.

It doesn't take me long to spot Rianna among all the other girls even though they are all wearing the same leotards . . even though they all have their hair pulled back tightly into a ponytail . . the palms of their hands all powdered like ghost hands. I would be able to tell her apart even if there were a million of them because she is the only one who would ever smile at the sight of me . . who wouldn't care about the mud on my shoes or the wild way my hair has been blown around in the wind.

She holds her hand up . . a quick wave before she steps onto the balance beam . . a quick smile to make her eyes into the shape of the full moon so that I know when she steps up there it will be for me . . when she moves the way angels move that she is moving only for me to watch.

She is not an angel though.

I know that now . . I know that it wasn't fair for me to ask her to become one either. She is more like me than like an angel . . and I was no better to her than people have been to me . . trying to make her something she is not . . trying to make her into what I wanted her to be the same way my dad would make me into a varsity athlete if he could.

She has her own secrets that make her want to hide . . that make her want to cover herself in dark sweatshirts . . that make her feel ugly the way I've felt too.

And maybe the both of us are too fucked up to be together . . maybe if we are together we'll only end up hiding together . . but I hope not. I hope that maybe it's more that we can understand each other . . that we both know what it's like to hide and maybe it's easier to come out from hiding if someone is there to wrap you up in their arms . . someone whose hands match perfectly over yours.

I'm the only one in the bleachers who applauds when

she is finished . . but instead of feeling self-conscious about the looks I get from the other people I give them looks back . . looks that I can tell make them all feel like maybe I'm right and that they should applaud more themselves.

I hear Rianna ask her coach if she can take a break.

He looks over at me to see who she is looking at . . takes a deep breath . . but then tells her *–okay . . ten minutes–* and she bites her lip to keep from smiling as she walks toward me . . as I walk toward her so that we can go somewhere more private.

–Hi– she says . . her head tilted away from me . . her eyes not willing to rest on me now that we are close enough to be able to touch each other.

–Hi– I say . . looking away from her too.

We walk quietly after that . . through the hall a little way until we get to the door. *–You want to go outside?–* she asks me and I tell her *–sure–* as she pushes the door open . . letting the sun swallow us.

–Rianna . . listen . .– I start to say. She puts her head down . . her hands holding each other as she studies the shape of her fingers and I can see in her face how much I hurt her . . I can see how much she knows what I'm going to say and is already trying to decide if she will forgive me. *–I didn't mean what I said . . not about you anyway. I shouldn't have said it.–*

She lifts her head . . her eyes disappearing in the sun as she looks out into the fields behind the school.

–*I didn't think I was going to see you again*– she says.

–*I know* . . *I'm sorry*– I say. –*I'm sorry*– . . saying it again because I will say it as many times as I need to until she believes me.

–*Sean told me what happened* . . *about the fight and everything.*– She blinks once at the sun again before turning to face me . . her eyes different then . . the way I remember them from across the classroom . . beautiful. –*He said you went home but that he didn't know if you were coming back to school.*–

–*I am*– I tell her. –*I'm coming back.*–

She smiles when I say that . . smiles because she knows she is one of the things that made me change my mind.

But then . . quickly her smile fades as she starts to speak again. –*Some of the kids have started rumors about you* . . *all kinds of things*– she says . . her hands relaxing . . her arms coming down to her sides inviting me to move closer.

–*Yeah* . . *I figured they would*– I tell her.

When our hands meet there is a moment when everything in the world ceases to exist . . a moment where we exist only in the white center of the sun.

–*Some of them started saying things to me too.*– Rianna

leans closer to me . . I can feel her heartbeat against my skin . . can feel the warmth of her body through my t-shirt.

–*I told them they didn't know anything about anything.*–

–*I'm sorry.*–

–*It's okay . . I don't care about them*– I see the little spark of sadness in her eyes again as I run my finger along her arm and up to her shoulder. –*I care about you . . and I won't let them say you're crazy.*–

And it's like we're out of focus . . like the rest of the world is clear and simple but we are blurred from it . . separate from it . . at least that's how it feels when our lips meet. We hold each other and kiss and don't care what anyone might be telling anyone else about us.

Because if we have each other then we have everything we need. Because as long as we make each other feel good about ourselves then we don't need anyone else to. Because if we have each other then we won't have any need to keep secrets . . or to hide . . because to each other we aren't as ugly as the rest of the world would like us to be.

–*I don't want you to leave me*– she whispers.

I hold her the way an angel held me once.

I hold her so that she can stop being afraid . . so she can stop feeling alone . . so that I can too.

–*I won't. I promise.*–

Before she goes back inside the gym she asks me if I will

come over to her house tomorrow . . tells me she wants me to promise I will no matter what.

–*What about your mom . . doesn't she not want me there?*– I ask.

Rianna comes close to me again . . her hand on my chest and she smiles. –*No . . but I do*– she says. –*Besides . . I spoke to her the other day . . I told her how I felt . . about what I said the other day. Anyway . . she sort of agreed that maybe she's been too strict.*–

–*So that means I can come over?*– I ask . . remembering the way her mother looked at me . . the way she made us sit on chairs on opposite sides of the room.

–*That means I'm saying you can come over*– Rianna says . . she says if I do then maybe she will let me kiss her again.

–*Okay . . I'll be there*– I say . . and she smiles.

As she walks into the gym I can only hope that when I talk to my dad it goes anywhere near as well.

I took the long way home on purpose . . walking down streets that I'd never been down only to see that they were exactly the way I've pictured them in my mind.

I took the long way knowing that at home something more difficult than walking was waiting for me at the kitchen table . . something more dangerous than a folded newspaper . . something more on my father's face than hav-ing read the news today because I know he didn't concentrate on the words printed there or on the box scores of the base-ball games played in other parts of the country. I know the only words he read were the words written in my notebooks even if they weren't printed there . . even if his eyes have never set sight on them . . because he knows them without reading them . . he knows them from Janet and I guess that might be harder for him than hearing them from me.

I took this road from the last road not knowing that it

would lead here to the park with the hill that wasn't made by rivers or mountains but was made by tractors and shovels instead.

I know I have to go home . . I know I have to face what I've put off facing for so long . . but I figure a little more putting off isn't such a bad thing.

I don't stop to stare at the people who are in the park . . it's just as easy to stare as I keep walking. I notice that they don't stare so long at me as they would if I looked away from them . . that staring them down is easier than hiding from them.

I notice the grass and the way that no matter how things change in my life the grass still smells the same . . only sometimes it takes more effort to notice those things . . to notice that children's voices sound more like small animals than like the voices of people . . that sometimes if you want it to the sun can shine brighter . . can shine closer to you.

She doesn't have to be here to be here . . for me to see her standing there at the top of the hill daring me to catch her . . because she's in here . . inside me . . always asking me to catch her. I think today that maybe I did . . maybe I only needed to catch my own breath first.

I run . . so sudden . . the change from walking to running with nothing behind me and nothing in front of me except the possibility of dreams that don't end with dog teeth.

I don't feel at all like a rabbit when I run.

I feel faster . . lighter . . braver.

The ground is there to catch me when I reach the top . . spreading my arms wide and spinning once . . twice . . like the propeller blade of a helicopter . . but not trying to lift me to the clouds . . to imaginary castles in the sky . . instead to ease me down . . to make a soft fall when I land.

The only thing to focus on is the white center of the sun even though I've always been told that it's bad to look directly into the sun. But it can't be all bad . . not when so many wonderful things can be seen there . . moving across the way images move across a television screen.

I can see us there . . different shades of white heat like trails that fall off from fireworks.

Rianna and me.

I can see us still when I close my eyes . . standing there in the impressions burned on the insides of my eyelids . . and I dream about all the different possibilities that could ever exist for us.

I imagine us at her house tomorrow . . her mother looking in from the hallway as we hold hands and imagine how maybe the sight of that might make them grow closer instead of growing apart.

I imagine us in school . . both small under the towering glare of lockers but close together so that we don't seem so small and not so intimidated by everything.

I imagine her competing in places all over the world . . always with a string wrapped tightly around her finger . . always with a smile that makes her freckles smaller . . always with me there with her.

I imagine what our kids might look like if we were ever to have them . . what we would name them . . how they would never have to show tiger eyes at us because I make a promise to myself that I will not be like my parents . . that I will always love them the way Rianna and I want to be loved.

I think of so many things and none of them surprise me.

The only thing surprising to me is that every one of them is happy.

I cross my fingers as all of the possibilities pass through me because that is a way that I can keep Lacie with me even if we are apart . . not her so much as her faith in me . . not so much for me but for her so that she will know she has never left me . . that I'm thankful for everything she gave me even if it seems like I'm not . . because it's not that I don't love her anymore . . it's just that I love her in a different way . . love her the way someone else might love praying . . love her for caring enough to try to save me.

I know there is one more thing I must do.

I know that none of these good dreams will happen until

I end the bad one. And I know he is the one that I need to help me . . that my father is the one I need to care enough about me if saving is ever going to be real for me . . because until it doesn't show in his eyes anymore I will always be damaged goods.

Healing

Most of everything my dad's ever said to me has been bullshit.

I guess that's kind of why I feel like talking to everyone else in my life first before him . . why I don't go to him as soon as I come home . . why I go into my room instead because I'm afraid he still won't understand me.

When he comes into my room I figure it will be more of the same bullshit that it's always been but that it has to get said anyway. I'm prepared for that . . prepared to let it pass as long it means he can accept me.

But when he sits down on my bed he doesn't roll his eyes . . he doesn't open his mouth to lecture me . . the only thing he says to me at first is that he knows he hasn't been a very good father.

I fold my hands under my legs and wonder if one true statement can cancel out all of the bullshit ones.

I tell him that I assume that means Janet told him what I told her and he looks away. *–Yeah . . she told me–* he says . . his voice like a small fire . . like the sound of a car engine dying as the ignition is shut off.

Neither of us can bring ourselves to look at the other one and so we both watch the floor and count time in our head . . wondering if there's a right thing and a wrong to say because we're both new at this . . we're both learning to be honest with each other.

And it feels different . . feels like there isn't as much space between us as there has always been. It feels warm . . but not the way a blanket feels warm . . more like the way a gun feels warm . . something that frightens me about the warmth because I know the cold won't come back afterward.

When he finally speaks all the guilt he feels is obvious in his voice. *–None of that's your fault Benji.–* And then he looks at me . . for the first time in his life . . looks to see me . . not seeing what he wants me to be . . not seeing the things about me that make me different from that . . but seeing me as I am.

It's not his words that have changed things . . it's not the two simple sentences that are significant. It's the way I look in his eyes that means everything in the world to me.

I don't say anything . . I don't tell him that it isn't his

fault either even though I want to. I don't tell him how I spent so long blaming him but that I don't anymore because I know there is nothing he could've done.

I don't say any of it because he doesn't give me a chance to . . because he puts his arms around me as soon as I open my mouth and I can't get any words out.

–*I'm so sorry*– he whispers . . his palm covering the back of my head . . my words lost in the fabric of his shirt.

It is the first time he has hugged me since I was old enough to remember and so I hold on . . I hold on the way I wanted to so many times before . . and I know he thinks I'm crying because of what happened to me . . because of the memories that have stuck around to haunt me . . but I already did that crying last night and this is something different.

I don't bother to tell him.

There's no need to tell him the difference . . the difference between feeling broken and healing . . that when you're broken you pull away and when you're healing you move closer . . I don't explain it because the only thing that matters is that he keeps holding me when I'm holding him.

–*We'll get through this . . whatever it takes*– he says. Then whatever he wanted to say after that gets choked up . . lost forever but it's not important because the important things have been said with his hands.

And even when he pulls away I can still feel him . . the safety of his arms around me . . that it will stay with me. Nothing else will matter after that.

I know that when I write about this later in my notebook that I will write about how this is the moment when I know I will be okay . . that no matter what happens I will be okay.

I will write down the last three words he says to me before he leaves my room. I will write down that he says he loves me.

I will write about everything that has happened to me and I won't tear out a single page. I will leave it all in there. I won't care what people think if they read it because I won't let myself be ashamed anymore.

I will write to Lacie and tell her how she has done more for me than she'll probably ever know . . and that even if we are not together I will always love her the same as when we were.

I will write Rianna a poem that I will show her tomorrow . . one that will show her the way I really see her . . one that lets her know she could never be ugly to me.

Then I will write about how I'm beginning to think that there are no such things as demons . . that what I thought were demons maybe were only angels in disguise . . because in the end the only thing they've done is to give me a father and a friend and a girl who needs me to love her as much as I need her . . and I will write down how I think maybe everything bad that happens is for a good reason . . that the bad things can't make us weaker if we don't let them.

Because deep down no one can take anything away from me.

I feel that inside me where so much emptiness had been.

Because I know something new now . . I know now that I am somebody.

It doesn't matter if I'm normal or if I fit in.

It doesn't even matter if anyone else sees it.

Because I know it's true.

I know there is nothing wrong with being me.

Brian James is the author of *Perfect World*, *Pure Sunshine*, and *Tomorrow, Maybe*. He lives in New York City, where he spends his time watching cartoons and collecting toys.